D1055437

Into Winter

Discovering a Season

Into Winter

Discovering a Season

William P. Nestor

Illustrated by Susan Banta

Houghton Mifflin Company
Boston 1982

Library of Congress Cataloging in Publication Data

Nestor, William P.
Into winter.

Bibliography: p.
Includes index.
Summary: A guide to the seasonal environment of winter, including activities and collecting projects, and information on plant and animal adaptation to cold.
1. Winter—Juvenile literature. [1. Winter]
I. Banta, Susan, ill. II. Title.
QH81.N47 1982 508 82-9232
ISBN 0-395-32866-7 AACR2

Printed in the United States of America
V 10 9 8 7 6 5 4 3 2 1

To Flo for her loving support
and to Bob Simmons and Roger Parrott
for their sharing, guidance, and inspiration.

The February Hush

Snow o'er the darkening moorlands;
Flakes fill the quiet air;
Drifts in the forest hollows
And a soft mask everywhere.
The nearest twig on the pine tree
Looks blue through the whitening sky,
And the clinging beech leaves rustle,
Though never a wind goes by
But there's red on the wild rose berries
And red in the lovely glow
On the cheeks of the child beside me
That once were pale as snow.

Thomas Wentworth Higginson
1918

Contents

Preface

Exploration of the natural world in winter begins in natural curiosity. The need to understand the interrelationships of plants and animals soon follows. The explorations increase our awareness of our own place in the scheme of things. These investigations, opportunities to see, feel, and understand, can develop in us an attitude of responsibility toward natural systems and lead to an enjoyment of the natural world that goes beyond spring, summer, and fall.

Winter is another season. A time of rest and dormancy for many plants and animals that is needed to prepare for bloom and birth in spring. A time of hardship that requires animals and plants to adapt. A season of travels and interactions told in tales upon the snow for all to read. Without winter, there would be no spring. Without summer, no fall.

Into Winter is a guide book for exploring a seasonal environment. It covers the animals and plants of the northeast and north central United States and southern Canada. This is an area of seasonal variation marked by distinct changes and true winter conditions. It is an area where cold, snow, and ice are an integral part of people's lives, where characteristics of the season are expected and enjoyed, and where plants and animals are adapted for survival in the harsh conditions. Yet, for most of this region the winter cold and snow are not so severe that it is impossible to explore and discover nature in winter. *Into Winter* is for children and adults in cities, suburbs, and the country. Although the animals and plants are specific to the northeast and north central United States and southern Canada, the activities are appropriate to any region where winter conditions are characteristic. Some of the activities will need adult supervision, but most can be done by children on their own. You can explore and learn about winter whether you live in a large city or a rural area.

In various chapters the suggestion is made to keep a journal. This is an excellent place to keep a record of which birds come to the feeder, sketches of insects found in rotting logs, or descriptions of various snowflakes and the depth of snow or wind speed on different days. It provides a source of information from day to day or year to year. Journal keeping is a rewarding way to record your discoveries. A loose-leaf or small spiral-bound notebook is good to use.

Use the activity ideas to find out about something you observe in winter, or as an inspiration to investigate this interesting season. Liberty Hyde Bailey, one of the founders of the nature study movement in the late 1800s, stated in 1905, "Winter is the best season of the four because there is more mystery in it."

Many people have been guides to my own wanderings through winter. These individuals have freely shared their knowledge and my excitement. They have encouraged my inquiries and exploration. They have valued my experiences. Their ideas, support, and friendships are greatly appreciated. Their guidance has, in time, shown me the way to interpret and understand the signs and information available to anyone who takes the time to explore, investigate, and experience the natural world. It is my hope that *Into Winter* will be a guide for others to discover what being "into winter" fosters in each of us.

Into Winter

Discovering a Season

Setting Out

As you walk in the woods on a January day, it may first appear a lifeless scene, still and serene. The quiet is broken by a noisy blue jay's harsh call. Its cry warns all other woodland creatures that you are present. Soon the "yank-yank" of a nuthatch adds a natural harmony, with the "caw" of a crow overhead. A flock of multicolored grosbeaks glitters in the winter sun as they move about collecting seeds. Chickadees flitter from branch to branch, always moving in search of seeds and insect eggs. A gray squirrel has left its warm nest in a large maple tree and now digs wildly in the snow, seeking an acorn cache buried in the fall, now covered by a foot of snow and leaves. In a nearby hemlock sits a porcupine busily chewing on the tender bark. A ruffed grouse has left its snowbank shelter and begins to look for buds and dried berries on which to feed. The plump brown bird walks easily on the snow. For winter travel it has grown scalelike hairs between its toes, which are like snowshoes.

The squirrel scampers up the maple tree and the grouse disappears behind hanging snow-covered hemlock branches. A stone wall, completely covered by snow, is now a long narrow mound. In summer, there would surely be a chipmunk darting in and out of the spaces between the stones. Within this wall, the chipmunk now sleeps. It remains motionless for long periods of time, awakening during winter thaws.

The woodland frogs, salamanders, turtles, and snakes are hidden as well. Many are sleeping in the ground below the snow, while others hibernate in the mud at the bottom of the pond. Many black dots are found in the snowshoe tracks. These are snow fleas, one of the true winter insects, active throughout the cold months. Hidden under bark, in decaying logs, in crevices of rocks and trees, or below the dead leaves on the forest floor are beetles and many other insect adults, larvae, and eggs.

A small clearing is laced with tracks of fox, snowshoe hare, and white-footed mouse. Brown goldenrod stalks stand out against the white background. On their stems are galls, which have been stimulated to grow by the activity of an adult fly. These galls now house the fly larvae for the winter. Another goldenrod gall has been punctured and the larvae it contained have become a meal for a downy woodpecker.

Deeper in the woods, a mother black bear wakes in her den to feed her almost hairless cub, now no larger than a chipmunk. The mother may have been here since November. She has stored enough fat to feed her young and remains inactive on her stored resources. The bears will not leave the den until April.

How do animals and plants survive through a long season of bitter cold temperatures, falling snow, and chilling winds? The ways in which they do so differ from plant to plant, and animal to animal.

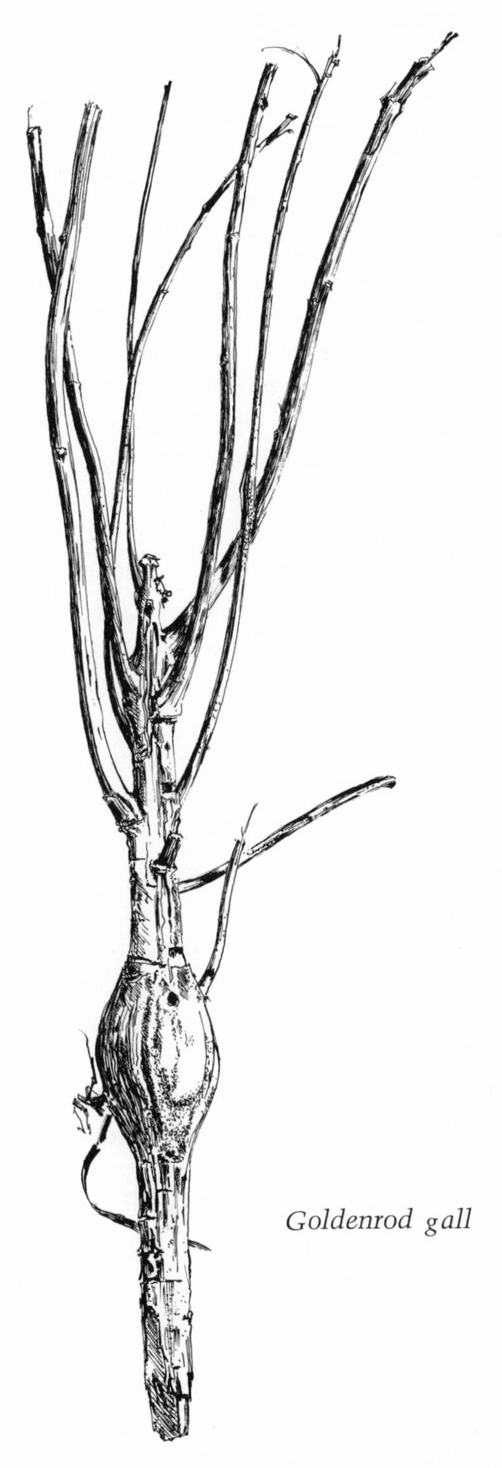

Goldenrod gall

Many of the activities in this book are done at least in part outdoors. Adapt them to your own needs. The activities assume you are willing to seek answers about the natural world around you in winter. Caution should be taken when doing certain activities. Read the directions carefully and ask for adult help when using kerosene lamps and when melting paraffin for the specific tracking activities. Be very careful when exploring water areas. Be certain to let someone know where you will be and always take along a friend. Never go onto the ice unless it is very thick.

Think about the clothes you will wear when you go outdoors. Dressing warmly is very important. If you're wet or cold, the experiences will not be as enjoyable.

Wetness is the greatest cause of discomfort outdoors. It can even lead to more serious problems. Hypothermia occurs when the core body temperature drops from its comfortable 98.6°F. The body responds to its first chilling by shivering in an attempt to produce body heat by rapid muscle movement. Warm drinks and clean, dry clothing are very important in preventing hypothermia. Frostbite occurs when bare skin is exposed to the raw cold for prolonged periods, and skin tissue actually freezes.

Layers of lightweight clothing provide warmth. Between each layer exists a small pocket of air that gives added insulation. An outside top should be of nylon or any material that helps to cut the wind. It is a good idea to wear woolen long underwear. Pants should be of a material that also blocks the wind and adds warmth. Wool pants are best, for wool has the quality, even when wet, of providing warmth. If the trunk of your body is warm and dry, it is much easier to safeguard your extremities from chill.

A hat which covers the ears is very important. As

much as 40 percent of your body heat can be lost through the head. So a hat is the key to a warm body. There is a saying, "Cold feet? Hat on!" Of course, there is more to warm feet than a warm head. Since your feet are continuously surrounded by wet snow, it is very important to wear waterproof shoes or boots, preferably mid-calf height. Wool socks keep the feet warm and dry. Mittens cover the other extremities, the hands and fingers. Mittens are much warmer than gloves. They should be of waterproof material, particularly when the investigation requires digging in the snow. Many prefer wearing woolen mittens and waterproof over-mittens.

1. Investigating Snow, Ice, and Temperature

Freezing cold temperatures, thickening ice, and blowing snow are characteristics of the winter season in the northeast and north central United States and southern Canada. Understanding these seasonal conditions and how they affect plants and animals is essential to understanding nature in this region. This chapter contains activities and information for investigating wind, temperature, snow, and ice.

Snow Crystals

The ice covering a frozen pond looks blue. Even ice cubes have a blue tint. But what about snowflakes? We all know they are white. Well, aren't they?

What do snowflakes look like? These crystallized droplets of water fall in a heavy storm at the rate of a million billion an hour on an acre. A man called Snowflake Bentley spent fifty years of his life studying snowflakes in the northern Vermont town of Jericho. Why don't you take a closer look at snowflakes, too?

Take a piece of black felt or paper outdoors on a day when it is snowing. As soon as the material becomes cold, the snowflakes that fall on it will not melt. Using a hand magnifying lens, observe the various snowflakes. What different shapes do you see? Try to draw them. Do this on a variety of days. Are the shapes different on different days? Keep a record of the weather. Pay particular attention to the wind speed, direction, temperature, and any other condition you think may be important. You may find it helpful to catch one snowflake and then stand under a protected area so other falling snowflakes won't pile on top of the one you are observing.

If you wish to make your collecting equipment more functional and permanent, cut felt pieces 3 by 3 inches and tie yarn or string to one corner of the felt so it can be worn around the neck. This will keep the felt cold, and handy for when you want to observe falling snowflakes. A spoon can also be used to catch and look at falling snowflakes, or a dark sweater or parka.

Although you may never find two snowflakes exactly alike, there are seven basic groups into which all snowflakes fit. Use the accompanying chart to try to find the group or groups in which the snowflakes you catch belong. Also use the chart to help determine if different types of snowflakes fall on the same day or if the weather affects the type of snowfall. How many types can you find?

How much snow falls on a given day? Why don't you find out? It is easy to measure the amount of snow that falls by constructing a snow gauge. Use a wide-mouthed can or jar. Put a ruler in the can, standing it up against the side. Punch two holes in the side of the can so that a wire can be used to hold the ruler in place. Masking tape can

NAME	SYMBOL	SHAPE
HEXAGONAL PLATES		
STELLAR CRYSTALS		
HEXAGONAL COLUMNS		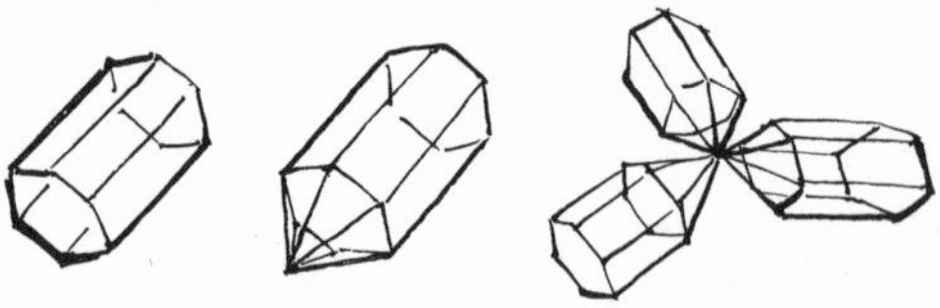
NEEDLES		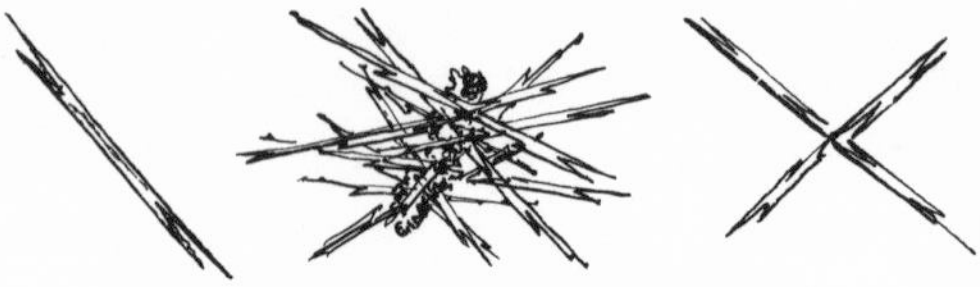
SPATIAL DENDRITES		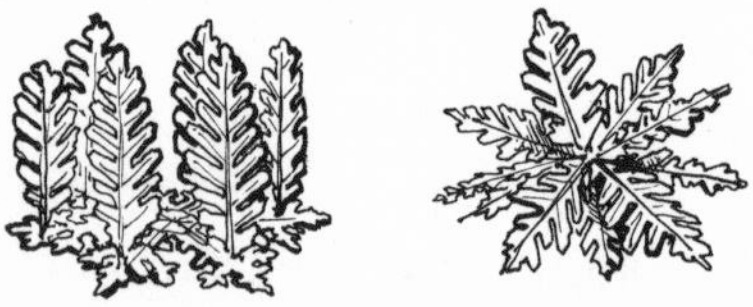
CAPPED COLUMNS		
IRREGULAR CRYSTALS		

be used on a glass jar. Mark the tape like a ruler and put it against the outside of the jar. The selection of a spot to place the collector is very important. It should be away from buildings or trees. Leave the gauge until the storm has ended to obtain a true reading. Read the depth from the ruler in the can or measured tape on the jar. If you take readings every hour, you can figure out the rate of snowfall per hour. Record the time the snowfall starts and finishes.

The most snowfall in a single season was 1000 inches, recorded in Washington State in the winter of 1955–56. How much snow falls in a season around your house? Check with the weather bureau to find out the record snowfall for your area.

You may want to place gauges in several locations to determine what affects various depths of snow in the same general area. Try placing them under a spruce or pine tree, under a tree with no leaves, and in an open field or playground. How do these different areas affect the amount of snowfall?

Another kind of snow gauge can be made by simply sticking a ruler into the snow. Record the level of snow where the surface level exists when you place the gauge. Measure the depth each hour or at the end of the storm as before.

How much snow will make 10 millimeters of water? Turn a coffee can or wide-mouthed jar upside-down and push it into the snow until it is packed full. Cover the opening with a piece of cardboard to prevent the snow from falling out of the container. Allow the snow to melt at room temperature. Keep it covered during this melting so no foreign matter can enter the container. How much water is left? How much snow is needed to make 1 cup of water?

Collect snow from different areas using the same procedure, covering the container and allowing the snow to melt as before. Pour each sample through a separate piece of paper towel or filter paper. What do you find? Do any of the snow samples contain dirt or insects?

Are the depths of snow different in various places around your house or school, or on opposite sides of a tree, on two sides of a fence, in an open field or school yard, under trees with needles, under trees without needles? In what areas in your school yard or back yard can you find varying depths of snow? With a friend or a group of friends mark the depth of snow in six different locations. Measure the snow with a meter stick or yardstick. You may want to use the meter stick or yardstick indoors. In that case tape a piece of masking tape on your pant leg to mark the depth of snow. Measure the height of the masking tape with the meter stick or yardstick when you return indoors. Record your findings on a graph like the one shown here. Discuss the differences and similarities you find.

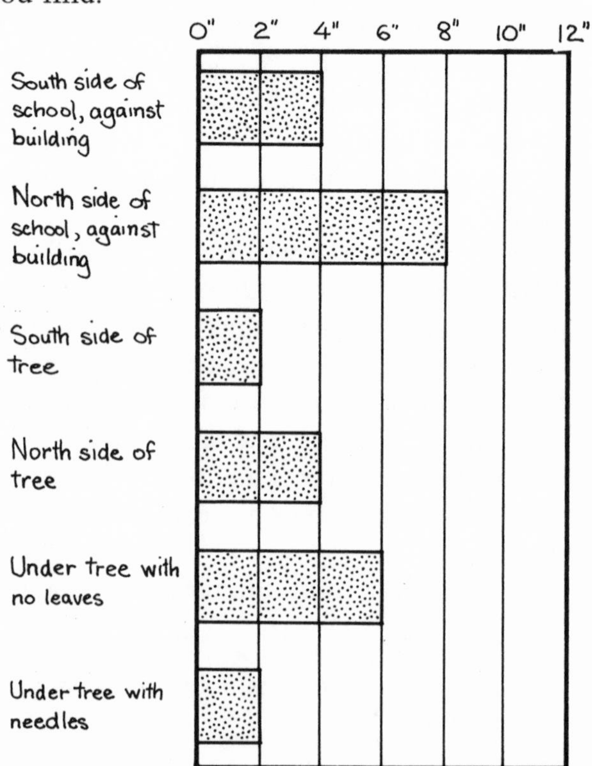

Temperature Differences

Does the temperature vary in different places on a winter day? To find out, go outside and stick a pole into the snow until you reach the earth. Using rubber bands, place thermometers on the pole at the surface of the snow, at 20 centimeters above the surface, at 50 centimeters above the surface, and at 100 centimeters above the surface (or at the top of the pole, whichever occurs first). Record the temperature readings on several days. Are the temperatures on each thermometer the same or different?

Try putting a thermometer into a rotted log or stump on a day when the temperature in the air is very cold. If you were a small creature looking for a place to keep warm, would you choose such a place? Find a hole in a tree and check the temperature inside.

If you find any holes in the ground, such as an animal home, tie a thermometer to a string or a pole and stick it into the hole. How does the temperature in the hole compare to the air temperature? To the temperature of the rotting log? Try this too after digging a hole in the snow.

Check the temperature inside piles of brush, leaves, or compost. Dig down under the snow until you reach fallen leaves and measure the temperature under the leaves.

Would animals want to find brush piles, ground holes, tree holes, or holes under the snow to spend the winter day? Why or why not?

Do different colors cause snow to melt differently? Place squares of felt or paper of different colors on the surface of the snow in the same area on a sunny day. Check them later in the day. Has the snow melted faster under certain colors? Which colors were they? Why do you think this happens?

Collect a piece of ice and put it in a tray or dish on a table. Place various objects such as a penny or button directly on the ice. Leave it alone for a while. Check it after 5, 10, 15, and 30 minutes, and 1 hour. Make observations and record what happens.

How long can you keep ice or snow from melting inside your house or classroom? What can you do to try to keep it from melting? How long are you able to keep it before it completely melts?

Collect a container of snow. Measure and record its temperature. Add salt to the snow and record the temperature again. Continue adding teaspoons of salt at intervals until the temperature no longer changes. Do this activity outside to eliminate any changes caused by the room temperature. What happened to the snow? Did the temperature rise or fall? Predict what will happen to the temperature before you begin. Why is rock salt spread on roads during a snowstorm?

Put the same amount of water in three or four similar containers. Milk cartons work well. Place a penny in one container, a small piece of wood or a stick in the second, a small rubber object in the third, and a small plastic object in the fourth. Put the containers in the freezer part of your refrigerator, or outside if the temperature is 0°C (32°F) or less. What do you think will happen? Observe what happens to the objects when the water freezes. Try the experiment again using different objects. What conclusions can you draw from observations?

Does hot water freeze more slowly than cold water? Place two cups of water—one containing cold water, the other containing hot water—in an area where the temperature is below 0°C. Label each cup. Record the temperature in the containers every 15 minutes. Which cup shows evidence of ice first? Why?

Experiment to find out if all liquids freeze, if they freeze in the same amount of time, and if they freeze at the same or different temperatures. Place 1 cup of rubbing alcohol, 1 cup of water, and 1 cup of milk (or any other liquid, such as juice, soda, or liquid soap) in three separate containers. Put the containers outside on a day when the temperature is below freezing. Record the temperature. Check the containers from time to time. Do all the liquids freeze? How long does it take each one?

Take a small amount of snow and find as many different ways as you can to melt it. How long did each method take?

Put equal amounts of water in a large flat dish and in a deep narrow jar. Leave both uncovered outside on a day when the temperature is below freezing. Which one first shows evidence of ice forming?

Did you ever notice how much colder it feels when the wind is blowing? Tape two thermometers to a cardboard shoebox—one inside the shoebox, protected from the wind, and the other on the outside, exposed to the wind. Can you detect a difference in temperatures between the two places? Repeat when the wind speed is different and when the temperature is different. What changes do you detect?

The combination of wind and cold temperature creates a windchill factor producing a temperature much colder than the actual air temperature. The chart on page 14 shows the effect of wind on temperature.

The temperature is determined by using a thermometer. But the speed of the wind can be determined by

Wind Chill Factor on Exposed Skin Area

TEMPERATURE (°F)	NO WIND	5	10	15	20	25	30	35	WIND SPEED MPH
50°	50	48	40	36	32	30	28	27	26
40°	40	37	28	22	18	16	13	11	10
30°	30	28	16	9	4	0	−2	−4	−6
20°	20	16	4	−5	−10	−15	−18	−20	−21
10°	10	6	−9	−18	−25	−29	−33	−35	−37
0°	0	−5	−21	−36	−39	−44	−48	−49	−53
−10°	−10	−15	−33	−45	−53	−59	−63	−64	−69
−20°	−20	−26	−46	−58	−67	−74	−79	−82	−85
−30°	−30	−36	−58	−72	−82	−83	−94	−98	−102
−40°	−40	−47	−70	−85	−96	−104	−109	−113	−116
−50°	−50	−57	−83	−99	−110	−113	−125	−129	−132

Take the wind speed and temperature readings on a cold day when a steady wind is blowing. Use the measurements collected and apply them to the wind chill chart. For a temperature of 10°F and a wind speed of 20 mph, the wind chill effect is equal to a temperature of −25°F. What would the wind chill effect be if the air temperature was 20°F, and the wind speed, 15 mph?

observing environmental surroundings. The accompanying chart provides a guide to determining wind speed by careful observation.

Another method for determining the actual speed of wind is to tie a piece of cloth to the antenna of a car. What is the speed the car is traveling when the cloth extends straight out? That will be the speed of the wind when the cloth is connected to a pole stuck in the ground.

Instruments for measuring wind speed and wind direction can be made with just a few materials found around the home. An anemometer will give you an accurate recording of the wind speed. A wind vane will indicate the direction from which the wind is coming.

Anemometer

Materials

Cardboard milk carton
Test tube, ball-point pen case, or cigar case
Four paper or plastic cups (cone-shaped ones are best)
Metal coat hanger
Colored crayon
Stapler

Procedure:

1. Straighten out the hook of the coat hanger and shape it as shown.

2. Cut four strips from the four corners of the milk carton. The pieces should be 1 to 1½ inches wide, so when the cardboard is folded each side will be ½ to ¾ inch wide.

3. Using a crayon, draw a circle around the inside of one paper cup.

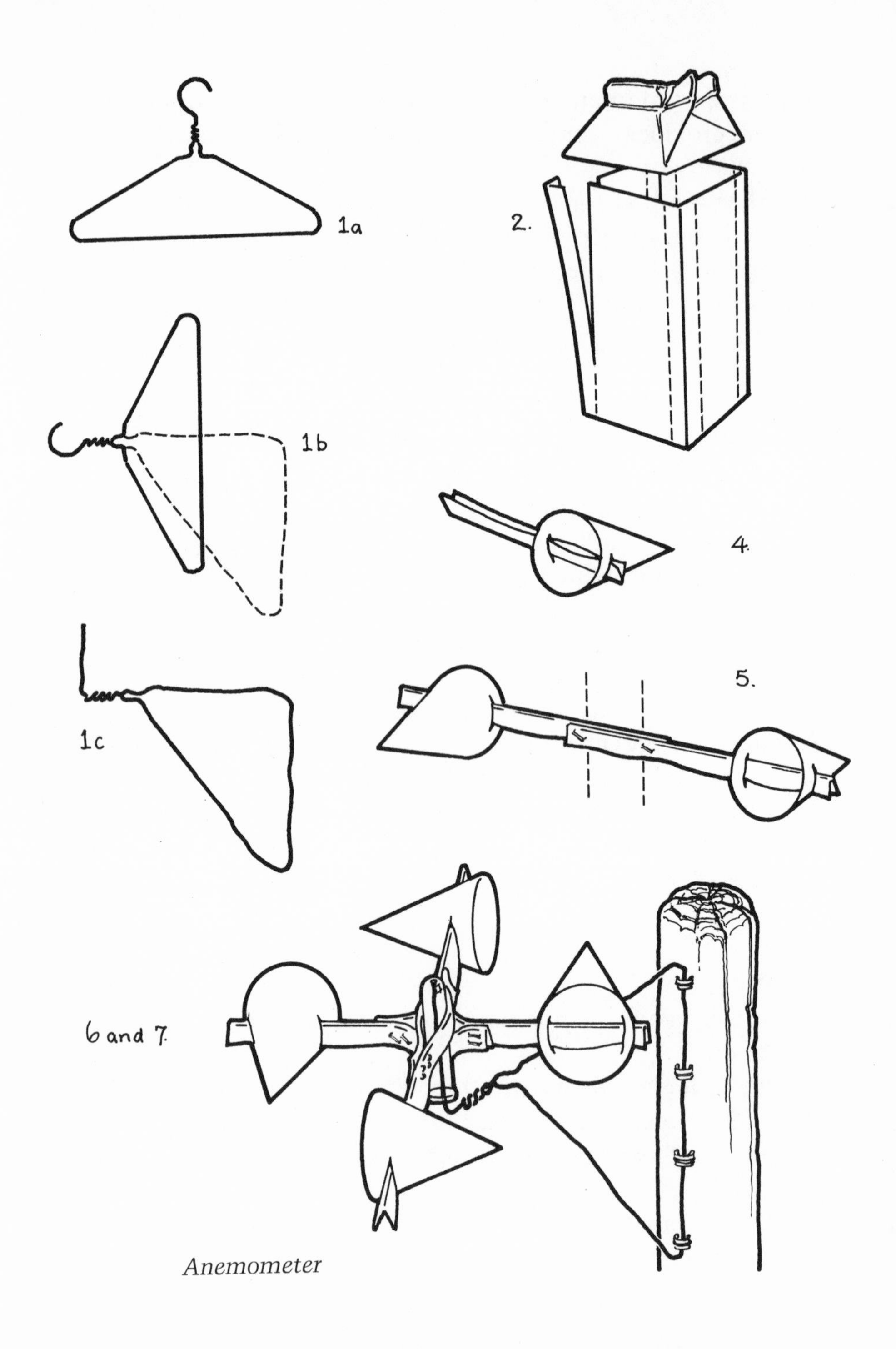

Anemometer

4. Cut slots about in the middle and on opposite sides of each paper cup. Make sure the slots are the same width as the cardboard strips. Slip one folded strip into each cup.

5. Staple the cardboard strips together, making sure there is enough space to slip the test tube through the opening made. Also be sure the cup openings are facing the same direction. Slip the test tube into place.

6. Place the test tube over the once-hooked end of the coat hanger.

7. Mount the anemometer outdoors in an open area by tying the bottom end of the hanger to a stake that has been securely placed in the ground. The anemometer will turn when the wind blows. To determine the actual wind speed, count the number of turns the anemometer makes in thirty seconds and divide that number by 5. The result will be the wind speed in miles per hour.

Keep records of the wind speed and windchill factor on various days. Does the speed of the wind affect the type of weather on that day?

Wind Vane

Materials

Wire coat hanger
Cardboard milk carton
Stapler
Test tube

Procedure

1. Cut out two arrows from the milk carton. They should be about 25 centimeters long, 10 centimeters wide at the widest in front, 5 centimeters wide at the widest in the center, and 7 centimeters wide at the tail.

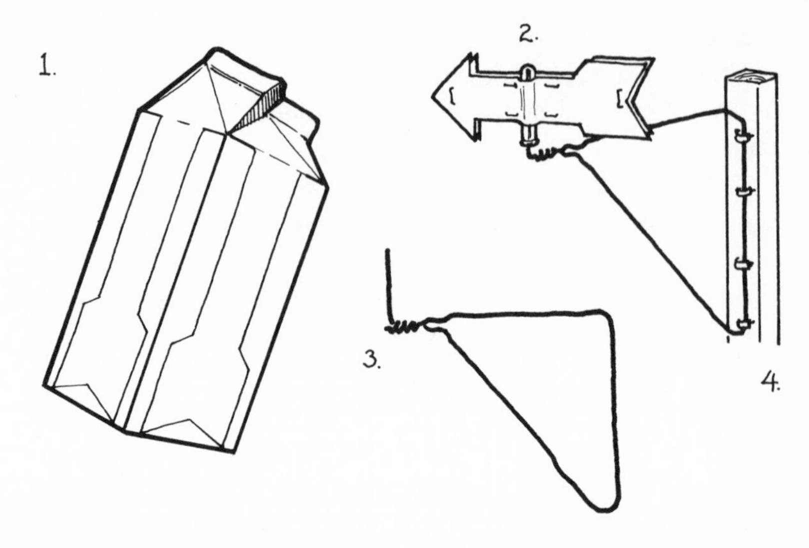

Wind Vane

2. Staple the two parts of the arrow together around the test tube.

3. Shape the coat hanger as shown.

4. Put the wind vane together as shown and mount it on a post in the open. The arrow will point in the direction the wind is coming from.

Try to determine if certain wind directions bring certain types of weather. Determine the wind chill and try to determine wind speed by observing smoke from smokestacks, a flag waving, or trees bending. Refer to the Wind Scale Chart on page 136. Is the wind speed greater at certain times of the day?

Does the direction of the wind vary at various heights above the ground? Build more than one wind vane and check the direction of the wind at various heights on different days.

Does the speed of the wind differ at different places in the yard of your school or home and at different heights? Measure the speed of the wind using more than one anemometer or by moving the anemometer after recording the speed of the wind.

Where near your school or home is it the windiest? The calmest? What month of the year is the windiest? Does the speed or direction of the wind bring particular temperatures, clouds, or weather?

2. Detecting Animals in Winter

Pretend that you just woke up on a January day, in a northern New England town. Last night's heavy winter storm has been replaced by a large mass of arctic air. The cloudless morning sky is crisp and clear. How will you dress yourself to go outside? What can you expect the weather to be like? What will you see, hear, smell, and feel on this morning?

A winter storm would most likely have left behind a snow-covered ground. The arctic air mass that brought a crisp, clear sky would also bring bitter cold temperatures. Winter days in the northeast and north central United States and southern Canada are often cold and snowy. Many areas in this region have snow on the ground from November to April.

The people living in this region expect such weather. They prepare for and adjust to the seasonal changes. Firewood must be split and stacked, storm windows put on, and snow tires mounted. Warm clothing, boots, and gloves are worn to maintain body heat. The demands of winter in the north country impose a way of life to which people must adapt.

Snow-covered ground and cold temperatures bring changes that animals must also adjust to. The snow and cold reduce or alter their food supply, and make it difficult to maintain body heat and to search for food.

How an animal responds to the changes in the temperature and food supply depends on its adaptations. Adaptations differ from species to species. These adjustments in activity and body are needed to endure winter stresses. An animal's adaptations make the difference between life and death.

Animals that live in the northeast and north central United States and southern Canada have, over time, evolved with adaptations suitable to meet the winter conditions of the region. The type of habitat and its conditions and geographic location determine the kind of animal that can live there.

For example, a red fox is mostly carnivorous in winter, feeding largely on rodents. In spring, summer, and fall, fruits and insects dominate its diet. If it was unable to adapt its diet to the available food source of the season, it could not live in an area of cold and snow.

Some animals migrate and thereby avoid winter

red fox,
pacing

stresses entirely. Others enter a period of dormancy that enables them to avoid a time of prolonged food shortage. Some mammals and birds remain active during winter. They must be adapted physically, or change their habits to ensure survival.

How do animals know when to begin migrating, preparing for a period of dormancy, gathering and storing food, or changing their activities? As winter approaches, the amount of daylight decreases. This is a signal to animals that winter is on its way. We are all familiar with the pattern of long, sunny summer days and short days and early nights in winter. The response of plants and animals to this changing cycle in length of daylight is called photoperiodism. Scientists have only recently begun to understand the effect of the exact length of daylight upon plants and animals.

If animals were to wait until it got cold it might be too late. The changing length of daylight is a reliable guide, consistent year after year, and one to which plants and animals have adapted and respond.

Fewer animals are active during winter than in spring or summer, and many of them are nocturnal. However, winter is the best time to look for mammals and their signs if you are a beginner. The secrets of their lives are clearly told and easily seen on the snow-covered ground. These signs give clues to who has been around, what they were doing, and where they have gone.

On page 137 is a partial list of mammals that occur in the northeast and north central United States and southern Canada. You can obtain a complete list of the mammals in your area by writing the state Fish and Wildlife Department, the local Audubon Society, or the natural history department of the nearest university.

Winter-Active Mammals

Winter-active mammals must have adaptations that enable them to survive the winter. Some are adapted physically, others change their habits. The fox changes its diet. The fisher and bobcat extend their range, traveling longer distances in search of food, most often roaming throughout the night and sleeping through the day.

Red and gray squirrels are active most of the winter but retreat to their nest during short periods of severe weather. During these times they rely on their cache of nuts and acorns for food.

Beavers cut branches and store their cache stuck in mud outside their lodge. This ensures a food supply when the pond is frozen over.

The long legs of moose and whitetail deer reach down through the snow cover to firm ground. When the snow gets deep (3 feet or more), even their legs are not long enough. At such times, moose and deer pack the snow in trails or yards, in an area with abundant food supply and adequate protection from chilling winds. This conserves energy that otherwise would be used up when seeking food. The snowshoe hare also packs snow to form regular runways if the snow is too soft and very deep.

The snowshoe hare and Canada lynx walk on the snow surface more easily, supported by oversized feet. Mice, shrews, voles, lemmings, and other smaller mammals seek shelter in nests under the snow. The weasel may come to the surface for short periods, while mice rarely leave their nests. Squirrels, mice, and voles gather and huddle together; their body heat is thus lost at a slower rate. Mammals that remain active above ground in winter have a much thicker coat of fur, adding a protective layer of insulation. The porcupine, who roams most of the year, feeding on vegetative matter, returns to a denning area. It feeds almost exclusively on the inner bark of trees and limits its range to within one quarter mile of its den.

Each animal has, in its own way, adapted to ensure survival in winter cold and snow cover. These adaptations suit the particular physical structure and behavioral habits of the animal.

Animals that remain active must be adapted to obtain food and avoid being food for others. The snowshoe hare,

snowshoe hare

weasel, and snowy owl utilize protective coloration. The hare's brown fur changes to white in winter, providing an ideal protection where snow exists throughout the season. Hares feed at night and rest in "forms" under the lower branches of conifers during the day. Their winter white enables them to avoid predators.

The winter coat of the shorttail weasel, or ermine, is all white, with a black-tipped tail. The ermine will sit with its tail in a hole and use its camouflage color to be a more effective predator. It blends in so well that an unsuspecting small mammal does not see it until it's too late. The snowy owl, white all year, leaves its arctic home in the winter to travel south during times of harsh weather or when food supply is low.

Try to find out which birds and other mammals in your area are camouflaged in winter. What do they feed on? Does their winter white help them to avoid predators or be better hunters?

Find out what each animal looks like, its size and shape, and information about its behavior.

Camouflage Game

Using papier-mâché, a stuffed white sheet, or silhouettes of shapes cut from white paper, make models of animals that are white in winter. Put them in the open or in a variety of places in a wooded area. Invite someone to try to find your camouflaged animals.

The time of day has an influence on certain animals' activity. When do you see squirrels or birds in the woods? Morning or evening? Find a sunny spot in the woods where there are many tracks and sit quietly for a while. Choose a time when you have noticed the most activity, or a time you think there will be much movement, such as early morning or evening. Most forest animals are very shy; sitting in a place where you are at least partially hidden will help you to observe more animals. If you sit quietly for a sufficient period of time, you should be able to watch animals feeding.

Take your notebook with you. Write down the type of food you observe each animal eating. You may wish to collect a sample of each type of food and make a display using yarn to connect the food sample with a picture of the animal that eats the food. Place the sample in a small plastic bag and label it. This will make it easy to remember once you have gotten it home.

Discovering Tracks of Winter-Active Animals

The winter is an excellent time to begin learning tracks and identifying the animals that leave their signatures in snow. From tracks you can learn which animals inhabit a particular forest, even though you may never see the animal that made them. Tracks are left by animals in many places. The best time for finding tracks is early morning, before the sun alters the tracks by melting them. The best conditions for winter tracks occur when a light, wet snow has dusted over a well-packed accumulation of snow, followed by a cold, clear night.

Use the accompanying drawings of some common mammal tracks and their patterns to identify the tracks you find. If the snow is deep or very wet, the individual tracks may not be clear enough to distinguish them from a similar species, but the *pattern* of the tracks will give the needed clue to identify them. If you would like to learn more about tracks, use one of the field guides listed at the end of this book.

Observe the patterns and characteristics of the tracks you find and also be aware of how many and what kind of tracks are in a particular area.

Different mammals move in different ways. The types of movements and their track patterns are described below. Try imitating the movements of animals you observe and attempt to discover how they make their tracks.

Pacing

In this gait both limbs on the right side move, then both on the left side. It is used by animals with comparatively long legs of about equal length, such as dogs, cats, foxes, and deer. The tracks of these animals are fairly far apart, forming a zigzag pattern. The tracks of the hind feet frequently fall in the tracks of the forefeet. See pattern A.

Diagonal Walking

In this gait the hind left foot and front right foot move, then the hind right foot and the front left foot. It is characteristic of animals with wide bodies and relatively short legs such as raccoons, beavers, skunks, muskrats, woodchucks, and porcupines. These animals, who walk along flat-footed, make tracks that usually form two lines, with the imprints fairly close together. When they move quickly, they go in small jumps, their forefeet and hind feet making paired tracks. See pattern E. Trotting is similar to walking except that the whole body is lifted off the ground at one point.

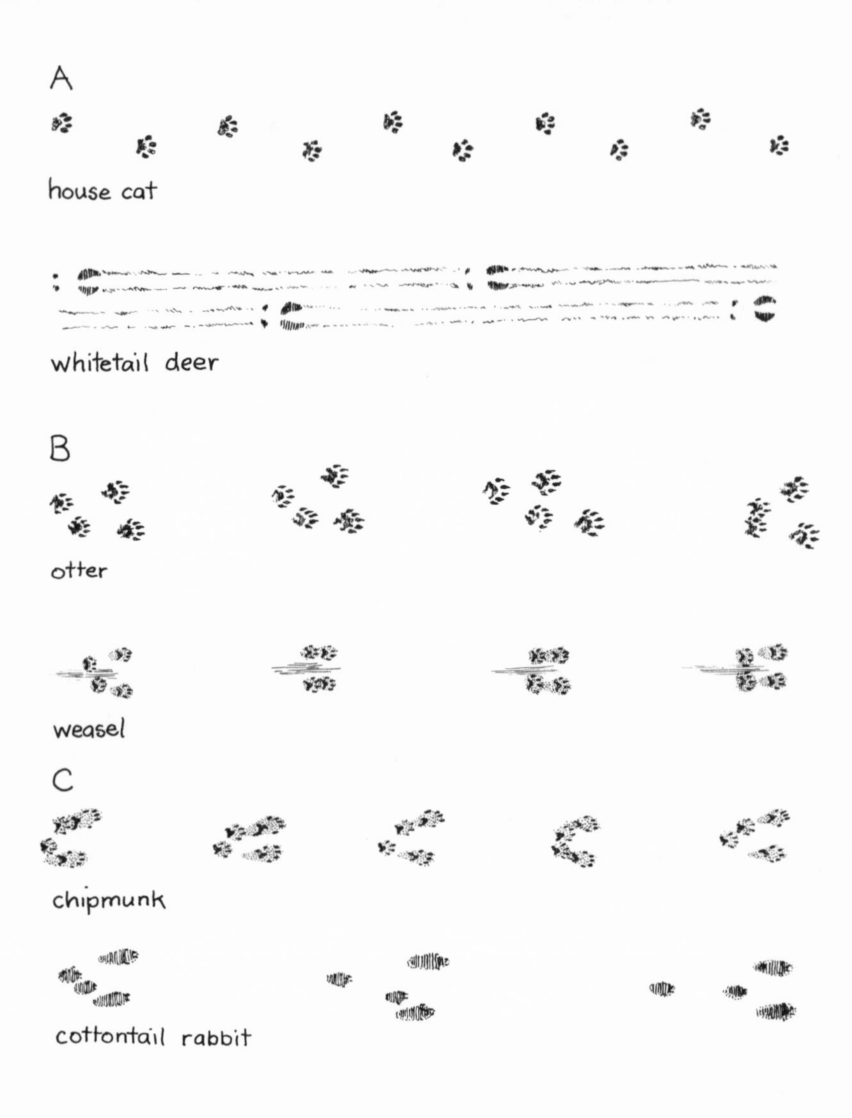

Bounding

In this gait the front feet go together and the hind feet follow as a pair. It is typical of animals having slender, long bodies with short legs, such as the weasel, fisher, mink, and otter. When these animals walk, the tracks of their hind feet are made a little behind the tracks of their forefeet. When they run, their hind feet often fall into the

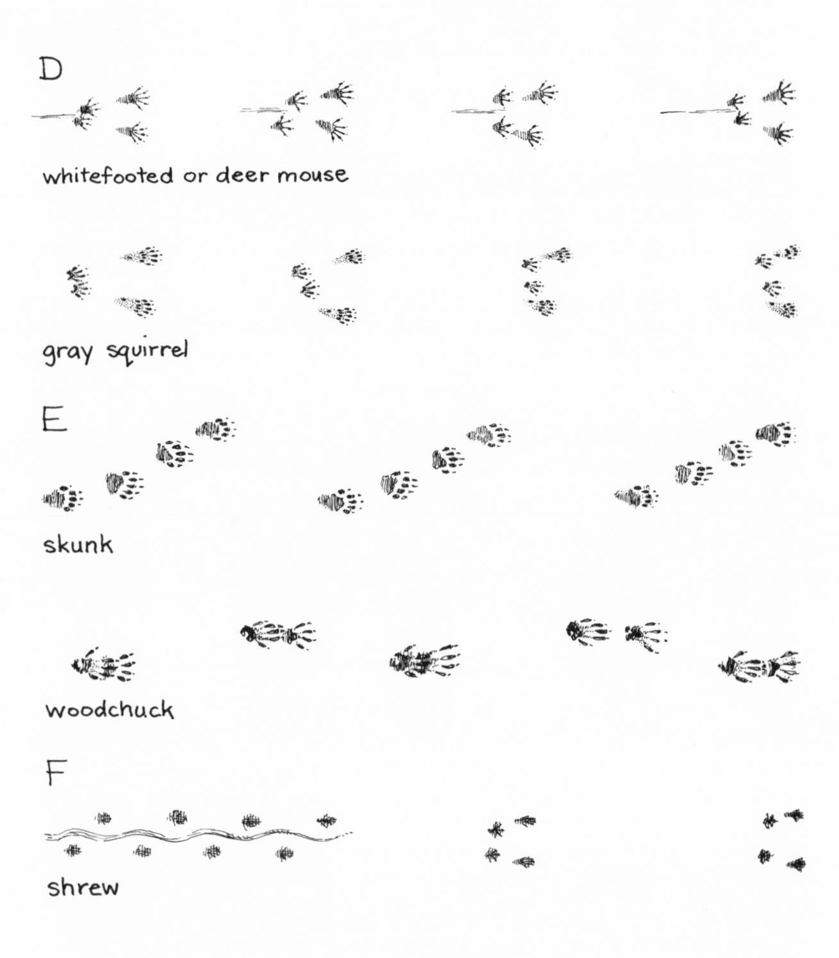

tracks of their forefeet or sometimes even a little ahead of them. See pattern B.

GALLOPING

This gait is similar to bounding except that the hind feet land to either side or ahead of the forefeet. It is characteristic of animals who have short forefeet and longer hind legs, such as hares, rabbits, squirrels, and certain mice. This track is also made by all long-legged animals (such as dogs, cats, and deer) when they are moving fast. See patterns C and D.

Running

Shrews and voles may gallop, but they usually run. Their tracks are a combination of running and galloping, similar to diagonal walking but wider apart. See Pattern F.

Guide to Patterns:

A: Fox, coyote, dog, wolf, cat, deer
B: Weasel, fisher, otter, mink
C: Chipmunk, rabbit, hare
D: Deer mouse, squirrel, raccoon running
E: Woodchuck, raccoon, skunk, muskrat, porcupine
F: Vole, shrew

Becoming a Track Detective

Get as much information as you can from animals' signatures left in snow. Ask these questions as you follow tracks:

1. Were the tracks made by a bird or mammal?

2. What is the size (length and width) and shape of each of the prints found? How many toes are on each foot? Do the claws show?

3. What is the pattern? How was the animal moving? What is the stride? Straddle?

4. Is there a tail mark? Was the animal short-legged or long-legged? Was it a fat-bodied animal?

5. Where do the tracks come from? Where do they go? Use a compass to find out which direction the animal traveled in. Where did the animal visit? Why did it visit there?

6. Are there worn or packed paths, runways or trails?

You may discover a different animal's track intersecting the set you are following, with signs of a struggle or the remains of a meal. A good track detective is always on the lookout for other clues as well.

Some birds and squirrels eat buds. Did any animals you observed feeding eat berries? Deer and rabbits "browse" on bark of young shoots and also eat buds. A deer has no front teeth (incisors or canines) on the top jaw; thus it uses its molars to tear and grind twigs. Rabbits and hares have both upper and lower front teeth and therefore make clean cuts. Look for twigs that have been browsed. Determine if they have been chewed by a clean cut, torn, shredded, or ripped.

Look for shells of acorns or nuts, which are a favorite food of squirrels and chipmunks. They enjoy seeds of evergreen cones as well. You may find cones that have been taken apart in search of evergreen seeds. Are there tracks nearby? Do you think the animal lives near the partially eaten nut, acorn, or cone? Do any tracks lead from the food remains to the base of a tree and stop? Can you find holes dug in the snow? These are evidence of squirrels searching for a cache of acorns or nuts buried under the leaves during the fall before the snow covered the ground.

Other evidence is left from feeding. Often, the remains of animal food such as bones, teeth, fur, or feathers can be found. Or there may be evidence of plant food that has been eaten, such as chewed bark, twigs, buds, and nuts.

Where do the tracks lead? Do they go to an animal's home? Homes are found in trees — abandoned birds' nests, or holes — or on the ground — in dead stumps, burrows, brush piles, fallen logs, stone walls, and snowbanks; beneath buildings; and under thickets and low-hanging branches. When you find a home, measure the size of the opening. What animal can use an entrance of that size?

Most fur-bearing animals have two kinds of hair. The first are inner hairs or underfur, which are short and dense. The second are outer hairs called guard hairs. The

Reading and Writing Track Stories

What happened here? Opposite is a story told in tracks. Can you read the track language to tell what happened here? (After you've studied the tracks, read the tale on page 135).

Using the tracks of animals found near your home, draw your own track story. If you find a track story in the field or woods, write about it. What animals did you discover and what did they do? How do you know? How good a detective are you? Try drawing your track stories on a window shade or long sheet of paper, so that when you unroll it the story will be revealed step by step.

guard hairs give the animal its color; often they can be found near entrances to homes or dens, on rocks, roots, stumps, logs, thorns, or even barbed-wire fences.

Are there any signs of an animal marking its territory, such as yellow holes of urine in snow, scat (droppings), disturbed areas, or sleeping places?

Each animal has scat of a particular shape and size. Scat can be useful in identifying animals in your area that you may never see. A field guide and patience will be necessary. Scat can also be dissected and looked at under a hand magnifying lens. Examination of the specimen will enable you to determine what the animal's diet consists of. If it contains hair and bones, the food comes from an animal source. The scat of the snowshoe hair, a vegetarian, contains partially digested plant fibers. Scat can be used to determine mammal populations in an area. For example, 4.5 pellets per square foot equals 1 cottontail rabbit per acre.

Track Story

Soft, light, or fresh snow will melt when warm scat comes in contact with it, causing the scat to sink deeply into the snow. The best time to collect scat, therefore, is when the snow has a hard crust. Animals often leave their scat under or near logs, brush piles, rock ledges, buildings, evergreens, entrances to dens, or in other areas protected from the snow and wind. Begin your search by looking in these places. Follow tracks in the snow until they lead to one of these places.

If you decide to collect scat, be sure to bring along small vials or jars. Let it dry for several days; then coat it with varnish. This will prevent moths and other insects from making a meal for themselves.

Follow the trails — they may tell a story about what the mammal did. Put together the clues of home, food, tracks, and scat to identify the animal. You can learn much about an animal's life habits if you can find the clues it has left behind.

Preserving Tracks

It is possible to preserve tracks and make a collection of those you find. Three methods are described here.

Extreme caution should be taken when melting paraffin wax and burning kerosene lamps. If these things are not done carefully, they can be very dangerous. It would be a good idea to have an adult help with these activities.

cat

PLASTER CASTS

The temperature should be below freezing for use of this method. Best success occurs when the temperature is between −18°C and −7°C (0°F to 20°F). Firmly packed snow that is at least 1 inch deep is best for this method.

Materials

Strip of cardboard (or milk carton with ends cut off) large enough to fit around the track, about 4 inches
Large rubber band or piece of string
Spray bottle
Coffee can
Plaster of Paris
Salt
Stick (for stirring)

skunk

Procedure

1. Press the cardboard into the snow around the track. Place the large rubber band around the cardboard to keep its form.

2. Spray water on the track. This will form a frozen outline of the track.

3. Fill the can half full of cold water.

4. Sprinkle in plaster of Paris until it has absorbed most of the water in the can.

5. Add one teaspoon of salt, to help the plaster harden faster.

6. Stir the mixture with a stick until it is smooth and even, like glue or melted ice cream.

fox

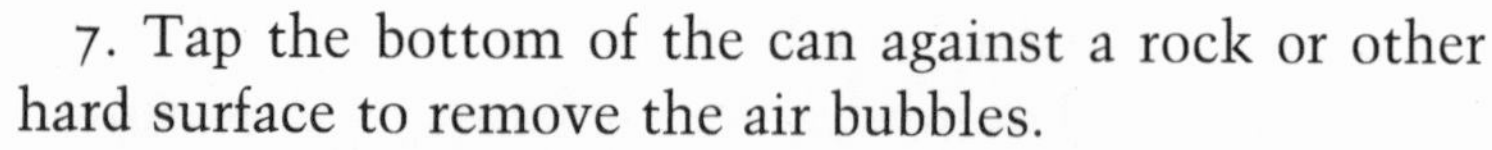

7. Tap the bottom of the can against a rock or other hard surface to remove the air bubbles.

8. Pour the mixture into the cardboard collar; let it set for 15 to 20 minutes.

9. When the plaster has set hard, remove it from the snow.

deer mouse

10. When the cast is completely dry, rinse it well and further clean it with an old toothbrush if necessary.

Paraffin Negative, Plaster Positive

Unlike the previous method, this is a two-part process. After you have made the paraffin cast of the animal track (steps 1 through 4), you can complete the procedure at home (steps 5 through 11). Remember, it is best to have an adult help with the first four steps, as Sterno and camp stoves can be dangerous.

chipmunk

Materials

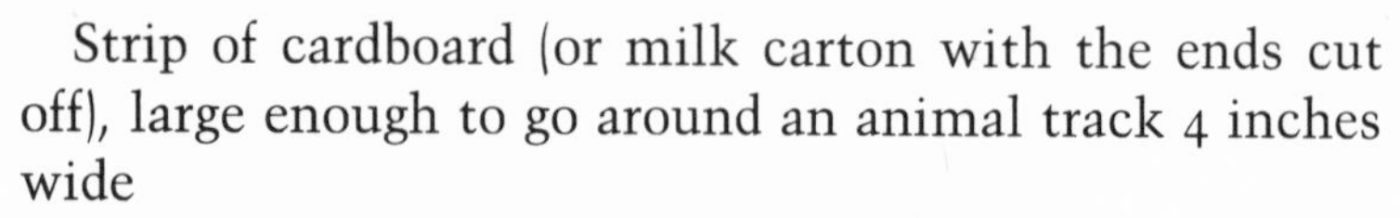

Strip of cardboard (or milk carton with the ends cut off), large enough to go around an animal track 4 inches wide

Large rubber band or piece of string
Paraffin
Small saucepan for melting paraffin
Pan for heating water
Can of Sterno or camp stove
Vaseline or other petroleum jelly
Coffee can
Plaster of Paris
Salt
Stick for stirring

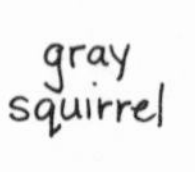

gray squirrel

Procedure

1. Press the cardboard (or milk carton) into the snow around the track. Use the rubber band or string to help

shrew

the cardboard keep its form.

2. Melt the paraffin in the small saucepan that has been placed in a pan of hot water. Use the Sterno or camp stove for heating the water. Let the wax cool briefly.

3. Pour paraffin slowly into the track, coating it completely with a thin layer of wax. It should freeze immediately without melting away the track, but only if you are careful not to pour in too much paraffin.

otter

4. Let the paraffin cool and harden. Then remove the cast very carefully, as it is thin and fragile.

5. Grease the cast with Vaseline. Put a cardboard collar around the cast, as before, and hold it in place with a rubber band or string.

6. Fill the coffee can half full of cold water.

7. Sprinkle in plaster of Paris until it has absorbed most of the water in the can. Add 1 teaspoon salt, to help the plaster harden faster.

8. Stir the mixture gently until it is smooth and even, like glue or melted ice cream.

woodchuck

9. Tap the bottom of the can against a hard surface to remove air bubbles. Pour the mixture into the collar. filling the paraffin cast to a depth of about ¾ inch. Let the plaster set for 15 to 25 minutes, until hard.

10. Separate the paraffin from the plaster of Paris.

11. When the plaster is completely dry, rinse the cast well and further clean it with an old toothbrush.

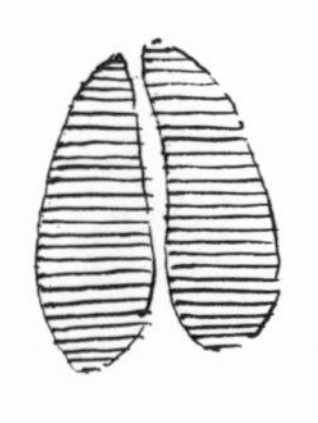

deer

Smoked Paper

Here again, be sure to have an adult help you, as working with a kerosene lamp, homemade or otherwise, can be dangerous.

Materials

Kerosene lamp (if you don't have one, you can make it

by piercing a hole in the lid of a small jar and inserting a wick)

Shelf or freezer paper, waxed on one side

Aluminum foil

Bait (such as apples, nuts, seeds, oatmeal, peanut butter, or salt)

Procedure

1. Light the kerosene lamp. Hold the waxy side of the paper over the flame (but not too close), moving the paper constantly to avoid a fire. Continue until the paper is evenly coated with black soot.

2. Make a canopy of aluminum foil to keep moisture off the paper when you take it outdoors.

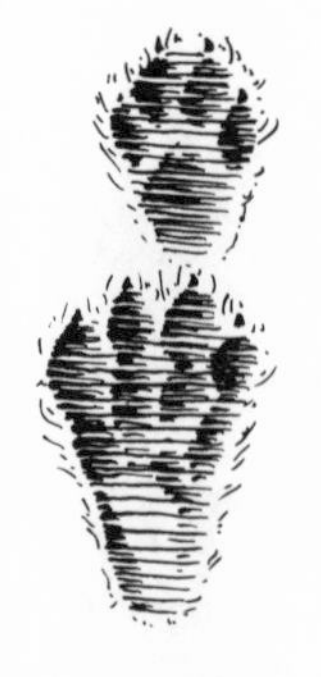

3. Place the smoked paper and the canopy in a spot that shows signs of animal activity — near shredded evergreen cones or partially eaten nuts, near an opening to a den or hole, or around a bird feeder. These are only a few ideas; think of other likely places. Place the bait so that the animal will have to cross the paper. When you return, you should find one or more clear sets of tracks.

Another time, you might want to try making a track trap for mice, voles, and small birds: Smoke the entire inside of a cardboard milk carton and place bait at the rear of the carton. Positioning the trap under a porch or overhang will prevent dew from settling, which would make the prints unclear.

Migratory Species

Migration is one adaptation to winter stresses. This seasonal movement from one region to another enables migratory species to avoid a reduced or altered food supply and cold temperatures. They select wintering sites where the conditions are less demanding and an adequate food supply is available.

Many migrate southward: seals, whales, and sea otter by sea; caribou and elk by land; and the monarch butterfly, some species of bats, and a multitude of birds by air. Some migrate only a short distance. Some birds that summer in the Great Lakes region, northern Vermont, or southern Ontario may only migrate eastward and south to the Atlantic coast or to southern New York or New Hampshire. Other species make a long trip that takes them to Mexico or South America. In many cases, the trip is thousands of miles. Other animals demonstrate vertical migration, leaving their summering grounds at higher elevations to winter in the valley below.

Dormant Animals

The photoperiod signals other animals to prepare for a period of time spent in varying degrees of dormancy. Winter dormancy enables animals to avoid starvation during a prolonged food shortage. It ensures cold-blooded animals (amphibians and reptiles) against freezing as long as they select frost-free quarters and remain there until danger of freezing passes. Their fat reserves supply a necessary source of food. They breathe through their skin when buried in mud at the bottom of a pond. (Insect adaptations to the problem of overcoming winter's harsh conditions are quite different. See pages 73 to 114.)

The decreasing period of daylight is also a signal to some mammals that pass the winter in a sleepy or sluggish state. Hibernation is a prolonged period of dormancy, experienced by true hibernators (deep sleepers) and winter sleepers (nappers). They begin a preparation period before entering sleep. Some store food, others grow thicker coats of fur, most accumulate fat by gorging themselves, and all prepare a winter home to protect against the cold.

There are few mammals in the northeast and north central United States and southern Canada that are true hibernators. They are the woodchuck; six species of bats (little brown myotis, keen myotis, Indiana myotis, small-footed myotis, Eastern pipistrel or pygmy, and big brown); and the woodland and meadow jumping mice. Some pygmy and big brown bats migrate, while others remain in their summer roost and hibernate. The small-footed myotis moves to a different cave to hibernate. The little brown bat migrates south, then hibernates. The keen myotis and Indiana myotis remain and hibernate in summer roosts.

The true hibernators go through drastic changes in body temperature, breathing rate, and heart beat. True-hibernating mammals have a greatly reduced body temperature, usually close to that of the surrounding chamber. The heart and respiration rate also are drastically reduced. The woodchuck's normal body temperature is 100°F, but during hibernation it drops as low as 37°F to 40°F. Its heart beat, normally 80 beats per minute, drops to 4 or 5. Its respiration rate of 235 breaths per minute drops to 4 to 6 per minute during hibernation. Similar reductions are found in the other true-hibernating warm-blooded mammals. Body functions continue, but are ten to one hundred times below the normal rate. As a result, the stored fat is sufficient to meet their bodies' energy needs.

Just prior to going into its prepared winter home, the woodchuck begins a fasting period. It will also feed on berries, which act as a laxative to clean out its stomach. The fasting results in a reduction of blood sugar, which causes a lower body temperature. The lowered temperature induces a further reduction in chemical activity in the body to match the available energy, causing unconsciousness (sleep).

Winter sleepers sleep through all or part of the winter. They display little change in heart beat, respiration, and temperature and remain inactive most of the winter. Some occasionally emerge on a warm, sunny day. Winter sleepers in the northeast and north central United States and southern Canada are the brown bear, raccoon, striped skunk, and Eastern chipmunk. The raccoon's winter temperature is 88° to 96°F, while its summer temperature is 98° to 102°F. Its rate of respiration and heart beat remain the same during each season. Skunks and raccoons show little change in heart beat and temperature, but a minor change does occur in their rate of respiration.

The Eastern chipmunk is included with the winter sleepers, even though some may enter a deep sleep for differing lengths of time. Researchers have found that about 30 percent of the Eastern chipmunks enter a period of true hibernation lasting 1 to 8 days. Some scientists think they are true hibernators, while others consider them winter sleepers. Eastern chipmunks dig deep and extensive tunnels with food-storage chambers at the end of each. The winter tunnel system, 2 inches wide, may go 15 to 20 feet deep and 30 feet long, with many forks and branches. Stockpiles of acorns and nuts fill the storage chambers. The animals select a chamber in which to sleep and fix the bed on top of a cache of acorns and nuts. Eastern chipmunks do not accumulate fat before hibernation; when they awaken periodically, they are assured an ample food supply.

Winter Sleeping Sites

True hibernators and winter sleepers must select sites that offer protection from below-freezing temperatures. A sleeping animal can freeze to death if the temperature of its winter home drops too low for too long a period of time.

Can you find places outside that would protect a winter animal from freezing to death? Test your choices by placing imaginary hibernating animals (containers of gelatin) in selected areas and noting how long it takes for the gelatin to set.

Any outdoor area is good, but one that has trees, bushes, mounds of soil or leaves, wood or rock piles, or hollow trees offers a variety of places and will be more interesting. This activity is easier to do with others helping.

Materials

5 film canisters (35 mm, usually available free from a camera store), or small (3 oz.) paper cups or plastic vials (Containers all should be the same size)

5 small paper cards (if you use containers without tops)

1 digging tool (hand trowel or shovel)

Liquid gelatin (1 qt. for every six people)

A watch with a second hand

Thermometer

Procedure

Choose a day when the air temperature is 5°C (41°F) or lower. Just before you are ready to begin, mix the gelatin according to the directions on the package. The liquid gelatin can be carried to the site in Thermos bottles and poured out just before each trial. Mark the cups or film canisters at half-full, to ensure that equal amounts of gelatin are poured. The temperature of the gelatin should be between 10°C (50°F) and 15°C (59°F) to start the freezing trials. When the air temperature is below −20°C (−4°F), you can use plain water that is 10°C (50°F) instead of gelatin.

Imagine that you are an animal looking for a winter sleeping site. Select a site and prepare it for your imaginary hibernator. Digging holes and using artificial building materials are permitted.

If you are doing this activity with others, be certain each of you places a gelatin animal in a different selected spot at the same time. To set up a control for this experiment, place just one gelatin animal out in the open. Visit the selected sites and the control site while you are waiting for the gelatin to set. Discuss what you think might happen. Which gelatin animal will set first? Which will be last to set? Try this activity a few times, and in several sleeping places. Which spot provides the most protection? Why?

3. Watching Winged Winter Wonders: Birds

Winter is an ideal time of year to begin studying birds. Most of the leaf cover, which in spring and summer provided hiding places, is gone. Also, migration has reduced the number of birds, making it easier to identify and observe the habits of those that remain.

A reduced or altered food supply, colder temperatures, and a shorter day are the stresses that all birds wintering in the north must endure. Snow covers food supplies and eliminates much shelter during a time when both are needed to maintain the birds' high body temperatures. Shorter winter days mean less time for locating food and feeding. Sometimes the entire day may be occupied with foraging. It would seem that the hardships are too severe for such small living creatures, yet most that remain survive and can be seen on the coldest day, some even flitting about from branch to branch. It is no wonder that people take such delight in feeding and watching birds in winter.

Flycatchers, swallows, and most warbler species, which depend on a large number of insects for their food, head south at the end of summer or in early autumn. In fact, approximately seven of every ten bird species leave New England in search of food and warmth.

The birds that do winter in northern climates can be divided into groups according to what they eat. Examples of insect eaters, plant and seed eaters, fish eaters, predatory birds, and scavengers can be found. Most bird species, however, do not fit neatly into any one group. These categories are man's attempts to create some order. The black-capped chickadee, a common visitor to the winter feeder, where it can be seen taking sunflower seeds, also feeds on insects found under tree bark. Actually, 78 percent of its winter diet is insects and spiders. The common crow eats seeds, insects, and fish; it also preys on animals with backbones, scavenges dead animals, or eats discarded trash.

Most seed eaters are equipped with bills that enable them to crush or split open their food. Seed eaters are the most abundant birds in the north during winter. Dried seeds remain on trees, shrubs, and weed plants throughout the winter, providing a plentiful supply. Some seed eaters, such as the junco or sparrow, prefer weed seeds, which they find close to the ground. Others, such as grosbeaks and finches, feed in trees and shrubs. Most plant and seed eaters have a tree, shrub, and weed source for food. That way they are assured a steady diet, even in times of deep snow. Many also feed on apples or dried fruit that remains on plants during winter. Blue jays, white-breasted nuthatches, and chickadees often begin storing food in October that they will eat in winter. The list of preferred foods on page 139 will be helpful when looking for a particular species of plant or seed eater.

The insect eaters find many adult and larval insect

forms in the crevices of tree bark. Spider eggs are another delicacy found beneath the corky layer of bark. Nuthatches and brown creepers have sharp, pointed bills for probing into such small places. Hairy and downy woodpeckers, whose equipment is even more specialized for food gathering, can also be found amidst this flock of foragers. Their bills are heavy and chisel-like, which enables them to chip into wood and excavate hibernating insects. Then, their long, barbed tongues uncoil into the hole and extract the slumbering morsel. Some of the insect eaters supplement their diet with seeds. Chickadees and nuthatches, for example, are frequent visitors to winter feeders, where they enjoy both seeds and suet. Next time you see a chickadee, notice its beak. It is short and sturdy like that of a seed eater, yet slender enough to enable the bird to probe for insects. The chickadee is a very successful example of adaptation. It has evolved to exploit two available food supplies. While three-fourths of the bird population must migrate, the chickadee remains a bright flicker of life in the winter landscape.

Predators such as hawks and owls feed by capturing many mice and an occasional bird. In many cases, the birds they prey on are weak, sick, or old. The predators are, therefore, a natural check against the spread of disease. (The term *predator* is usually reserved for those animals that feed on other animals having backbones.) Many birds of prey migrate because their food source is less abundant in winter, but some remain. Others whose normal wintering grounds are Canada or far north in the United States may winter farther south during years when their food supply is not adequate. For example, the snowy owl's primary food supply is the lemming. Every four to seven years the lemming population drops off. During these times this white (and the largest) owl, an active daytime feeder, winters far south of its arctic home. In some years, there is an influx of the snowy and other northern owls. Listen for reports of these beautiful winter visitors. The red-tailed hawk is a bird of prey that regularly winters in the north and can be observed soaring over open fields in search of food. Rabbits, squirrels, small rodents, and birds are the most common winter prey for these birds.

On page 141 is a list of birds that can be found in parts of the northeast and north central United States and southern Canada during winter. This list is not necessarily complete, and some birds may not occur in your immediate area. For a complete list for your town, contact your local Audubon Society.

Keeping a journal will provide information about the birds you see and the behavior they exhibit. These observations will be your permanent record, which can be compared and referred to from day to day, throughout the winter season, as well as from year to year.

In order to be able to identify birds, you must be familiar with the body parts. The accompanying drawing explains those parts. When you are making your observations, pay particular attention to the size and shape of the beak, crest, wings, tail, and feet.

Guidelines for Field and Feeder Observation

Much can be learned from observations of birds and their behavior. Whether you see a bird at a feeder or in the field, take note of these characteristics.

Size

Is the bird larger or smaller than a sparrow (15 centimeters long), a robin (25 centimeters long), a crow (50 centimeters long)?

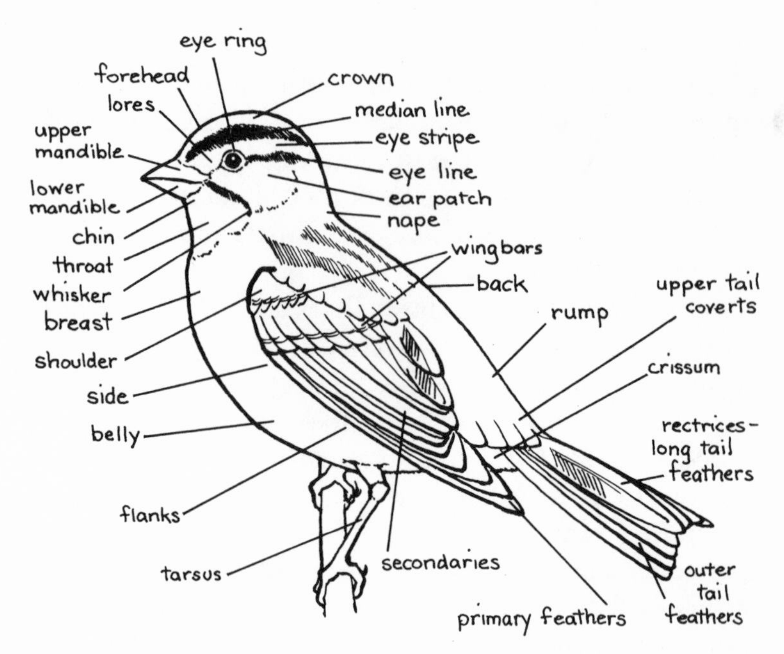

Parts of a Bird (White-throated Sparrow)

Shape

Body: Is it plump, thin, short and stubby, streamlined?

Head and Bill: Is the bill thick or slender, long or short? Is there a crest or not?

Tail: Is it notched, rounded, square?

Wings: Are they pointed, rounded?

Legs: Are they long, short?

Coloring

What color are the wings, belly, throat, feathers, and tail?

Habitat

Is the bird at the top of a tree, on the ground, in bushes, a wooded area, marsh? Is it on an electrical wire, a fence post, a tree trunk, small branches?

Behavior

Is it eating, preening its feathers, drilling, collecting seeds or insects, swimming? Is it solitary, in a flock or small group? Is its flight pattern jerky, swooping, darting?

Things You Can Do To Learn About Birds in Winter

Find feathers left by birds. What is the structure of the feather? Most feathers left by birds are contour feathers. They include the feathers of the wings and tail, and also form the outer covering of the bird's body. Using a magnifying lens, examine a feather. It has a central hollow shaft running its entire length. On each side of the shaft is a flat surface with many interlocking rows of barbs.

Observe the flight patterns of a variety of birds. Do they fly the same or differently? Do any birds you observed fly in a pattern like any of the drawings on p. 50?

Write a story about what you think it would be like to be a specific bird in the winter.

Construct a papier-mâché model of a regular winter visitor to your bird feeder.

Draw or sketch the birds that visit your feeder and also those you see at other places in the winter.

Observe differences and similarities of the feet of various birds. Are there two toes in front and two behind, or three in front and one behind? Are they webbed? How do the birds' feet relate to or affect their feeding habits?

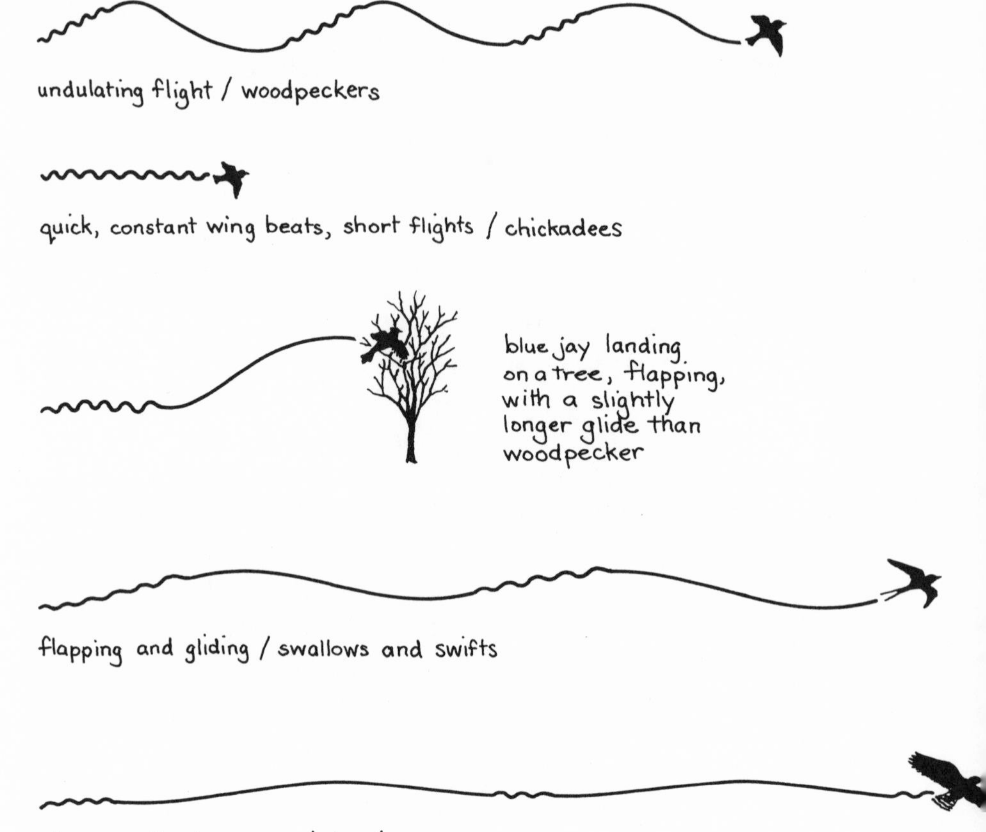

Flight Patterns

Feeding and Feeders

The best time to begin a feeding program is in the early fall. Most birds that are going to winter in your area start locating reliable sources of food during this time. Once you begin feeding, it is very important that you continue until well into spring, when birds can again obtain their food from natural sources. Although they probably can get a sufficient amount of food on their own, they will become dependent on your supply. If you do not intend to keep food available continuously, do not begin a feeding program. Irregular feeding may cause unnecessary hardship and possible death to the birds.

Most birds have specific food preferences. Many visit feeders in search of one food type. Therefore, to attract a variety of birds, a wide selection of food should be supplied.

Birds that visit feeders can be divided into three groups.

1. Seed-eating birds (such as the tree sparrow) that feed on or near the ground. They eat grain and small seeds and prefer food that was thrown or has fallen to the ground. They will occasionally come to platform feeders.

2. Seed-eating birds (such as the purple finch and evening grosbeak) that prefer to feed 4 to 5 feet above the ground. Feeders for these birds should be hung from a tree or mounted on a pole.

3. Insect-eating birds such as chickadees, woodpeckers, and nuthatches, which prefer to feed above the ground. Suet or peanut butter is a substitute for insects, spiders, larvae, and eggs.

On page 143 is a list of some common visitors to winter feeders.

Begin feeding with a commercial bag of mixed seed. The mixture should contain millet, other small seeds, cracked corn, some peanut hearts, and sunflower seed. As you observe the various birds dining at your feeder, you can determine their preferences. Sunflower seeds are a favorite of many species. Because of their popularity, you may want to fill one of your feeders with only sunflower seeds. They are eaten eagerly by chickadees, blue jays, nuthatches, tufted titmice, cardinals, evening grosbeaks, purple finches, and others.

A tray or platform feeder is easy to make. A raised edge will prevent seeds from being knocked off or blown away. A roof will give added protection from wind and rain. The platform tray can be set on a pole, attached to a windowsill, or placed on a stump. A sill feeder enables you to watch birds closely, but some are very timid and may not feel comfortable near a building. Therefore, a tray feeder on a pole some distance from the house is best for them. It is ideal to have one of each.

Birds come to feeders if cover or shelter is nearby. Shrubs or trees within a few feet of a feeder satisfy this need. A brush pile serves the same purpose. Visitors to feeders prefer a place to feed in the sun and out of the wind. The best location therefore, is a sheltered southern exposure. Experiment and place feeders in various places around your home or school.

Before constructing a feeder, make a scale drawing. Determine the amount of lumber and other materials you will need.

Spreading seed on the ground near the feeder will help the birds find it more quickly. A group of birds will attract others; once the food source is located by some, a variety of species may soon appear.

Even on days when it may be too cold to go outside, you can discover the similarities and differences of birds' behavior and food preferences. Birds display a variety of behaviors which can be observed at feeders during winter. Some are calm, and can be approached closely; others are nervous and fly off at the slightest nearby movement.

The ways that different species come to the feeder are many and varied. The white-breasted nuthatch approaches the feeder with a roller-coaster flight. It lands on the upswing. Like the chickadee, it would rather open the seeds in a nearby tree or shrub. Chickadees dash in quickly, grab a sunflower seed, and take it to a nearby branch to hull the shell and take out the kernel. After they have become accustomed to the feeder, they may sit on the edge when it is not occupied and open many seeds, one right after another. One feeder in a open area facing south in front of my house is regularly visited by chickadees. This is a hanging feeder, frequented by a variety of birds (mourning doves, evening grosbeaks, juncos, tree sparrows) that feed on the ground, from the feeder, and from the ripened fruit of the crabapple trees. The chickadee will seldom stay and feed at this feeder, but another one, on the north side of the house and not often frequented by large mixed flocks, has chickadees sitting on its edge, repeatedly eating sunflower seeds. The nuthatch, like the blue jay, will store unopened seeds in tree cavities or bark crevices. It begins gathering seeds early in the fall for later feeding. Tree sparrows, white-throated sparrows, and dark-eyed juncos can often be seen peacefully picking small seeds from the ground among the shrubs just behind the feeder. Mourning doves will settle in pairs or more and docilely feed from smaller seeds strewn about the ground. Redpolls and evening grosbeaks will overtake the feeder in flocks. Evening grosbeaks will land on a platform feeder and aggressively shell seed after seed without moving. Blue jays fly in, colorful and noisy as if to announce their arrival. They will dominate the feeder, occasionally driving off other birds with a direct aggressive act. More often, other species will immediately yield to their presence and leave the feeder upon the jays' arrival.

A suet feeder on the trunk of a tree will attract birds who are not seed eaters. Methods of approach differ here as well. Chickadees and jays fly right to the suet. The nuthatch lands above the suet and approaches head down to feed. Hairy and downy woodpeckers and brown creepers have distinctive manners of approach. Watch closely and learn their ways. Suet can also be tied to the branch of a tree or a window feeder. (See the box on page 55 for directions about preparing suet for birds.)

A bit of peanut butter spread on cracks of bark or at the feeder will attract the insect-eating suet lovers. Peanut butter, like suet, is protein rich. Try adding whole peanuts to the peanut butter.

The way in which birds eat also varies with species and individual birds. Opening a sunflower seed is done in various ways. The chickadee holds the seed between its feet and hammers away with its pointed bill. The nuthatch wedges it into a crevice and then opens it. The nuthatches may then carry seeds away to store in crevices or under bark, where they are often found and stolen by other nuthatches, jays, or chickadees. The bills of chickadees and nuthatches are thin and sharp, unlike those of cardinals and finches, which turn the seeds in their larger, stronger bills and force open the seeds. They hull the sunflower seed, keeping the kernel, and then spit out the shells. Evening grosbeaks crush the seeds with their powerful bills, opening them as fast as they pick them up. Blue jays have little difficulty with sunflower seeds, opening them easily. If in a rush, they will swallow them whole, one after another.

Depending upon the number and variety of species visiting your feeder at any one time, a pecking order can be observed. Blue jays and grosbeaks are often dominant species. Other birds will leave entirely, or be content to feed on the fringe of a dominant group of birds. This order is easily observed and is an interesting behavior pattern that you should look for.

It is very rewarding to watch birds at your feeder, especially knowing that you are responsible for its construction and food preparation. There also are times when you'd like to get a little closer to the feeding birds.

How to Make Suet-able Food for Insect Eaters

Insect-eating birds require a source of protein throughout the winter. If you would like to attract woodpeckers, nuthatches, or chickadees, provide suet, which is the fat surrounding kidneys of cattle and sheep. It can be purchased from the butcher, and is relatively inexpensive. The suet can be cut into large pieces and hung in onion bags. Another method is to cut it into small pieces or put it through a meat grinder. This will allow the suet to be melted into a smooth lump. Heat the cut or ground pieces in a double boiler. When it is completely melted, let it cool and harden. Remelt the suet and pour it into small aluminum dishes, holes drilled in a slender log, orange or grapefruit skins, or another container.

You can make suet-seed cakes by pouring remelted suet over mixed seeds, raisins, oatmeal, cracked corn, uncooked rice, or sunflower seeds that have been placed in aluminum trays, fruit skins, or coconut shells. Try other ingredients. Make up your own combinations. You can fill the holes of a suet log with the mixture or smear it on dead tree limbs.

Kitchen fat can also be used as bird food. Collect the fat in a can until a quantity has been accumulated. Stir in cornmeal, flour, and other ingredients such as chopped nuts, seeds, and raisins. This can be placed in a container or smeared on the bark of trees.

Some birds enjoy peanut butter and actually prefer it to suet. It can also be combined with seeds or other ingredients, but it is much more expensive than suet.

This can be done by two methods. The first is to build a feeder partially inside and partially outside your window. If it is made of clear plastic, you will see birds actually feeding within your own home. Placing moss or soil on the bottom of your feeder will make the atmosphere a bit more comfortable for the visiting diner.

The second method allows you to have birds eat out of your hands. Make a scarecrow and a tray feeder. Secure the scarecrow just behind the feeder tray so its hands actually rest on the tray. Let the birds become accustomed to and comfortable with the scene. After they come and go at will, put on the scarecrow's clothing; then take its place. Rest your hands, filled with seed, on the feeder tray. It is an exciting experience to have these fragile living things land and feed on you, a living bird feeder. If your hands are open, with the palms up, the birds may even feed right out of them.

You can make your own bird-watching binoculars from a pair of empty toilet-paper tubes. Tape one end of a neck strap (leather, twine, or yarn) to each tube. Paint the tubes any color or combination of colors you'd like. Slip rubber bands around both ends or tape the tubes together. These binoculars enable you to get used to a narrow field of vision, so the experience with real binoculars will not be as frustrating.

Here are some additional feeder-related activities.

What is this seed? Separate the different kinds of seeds you have been feeding the birds and place the groups between wet newspaper. Leave them for a few days, keeping the newspaper wet. When they begin to sprout, plant each group in a separate container. Observe the rate of growth. Compare the height, texture, and smell of each variety. What does each grow to become?

How much do birds eat? Weigh the feed and keep a record of the daily amount put in each feeder. Keep records of the daily weather factors that you feel are important: temperature, wind speed and direction, barometric pressure, snow, rain, length of day, cloudy, clear, and so on. Does the weather affect the amount of food eaten daily?

What do specific species eat? Suet, large seeds, small seeds? How do they eat? (Crack with bill, hold in feet

against a limb and crack?) Does the size and shape of the bill have any relationship to their diet and how they eat? Does the bird swallow seeds whole, crack them, pick at suet, or eat in another way? Watch closely and see.

Where does a certain kind of bird feed? On the ground, on a tree, at the feeder? Does it feed in groups or individually? Does it frighten easily or is it bold? Does it fly directly to the feeder or stop nearby and then continue to the feeder? Will one bird species feed together with another species? Do any other animals come to the feeders? What behavior do they display?

4. Discovering Plants in Winter

Unlike animals, plants have no alternative but to remain stationary. As a result, they have, over time, acquired adaptations to survive the stresses of seasonal changes.

What are these stresses that woody and herbaceous plants must endure to survive? How are they adapted to do so?

Snow, ice, dry winds, and cold temperatures can create a difficult time for plants in winter. Individual species differ in their ability to withstand them. To a great extent, these stresses determine the make-up of natural communities in the northeast and north central United States and southern Canada. The climate in a given area determines the plant life, which in turn helps to determine the soil type. The climate, plant life, and soil determine the kinds and numbers of animal species in a given community.

Snowfall may bury many plants. Freshly fallen snow acts like a goose-down jacket. It wraps air over sensitive plant tissues and forms an insulating cover. Snow is particularly valuable in protecting a plant from wind. The freezing winds sometimes drive abrasive bits of hard snow and ice that scour vegetation. A more serious effect is drying of plants caused by constant winds. Since the top layer of soil is frozen in the winter, moisture is sealed off from reaching plant roots. So winter is not only a time of bitter cold, but one of extreme drought for plants. Water that evaporates from plant surfaces is not replenished through the roots as it is during the other seasons.

Herbaceous (nonwoody) plants grow to a relatively small size and have a simple yet efficient means of wintering over. Annuals (such as the daisy) die back in winter, but new plants grow the next season from seeds. Biennials (the mullein, for example) grow vegetative parts the first year and in some species winter over as a rosette of leaves under the snow. The second year's growth produces flowering parts that go to seed. The second winter is spent as seeds. Perennials (like the dandelion) die back to the ground during winter. Their root remains underground and produces a new growth of flowering parts and seeds year after year. Many of these herbaceous plants' dried remains can be observed in winter.

Some fern species remain green all year. They provide a contrast to the browns of bark and dried leaves. They are much easier to see when trees have lost their green leaves. Some that are commonly found are Christmas ferns. Their individual leaflets are shaped like Christmas stockings. Also prevalent in winter are the woodfern, with its more delicate fronds, the polypody (found in crevices of rocks and cliffs), and the spore fronds of the sensitive fern.

The woody plants — trees, shrubs, and woody vines — remain alive above the ground during winter. Some plants that would die at just below freezing in August can withstand temperatures as low as −196°C in winter. They have adapted to exist in a dormant state.

In order for woody plants to survive, a change from a tender condition to a hardy condition naturally occurs. They undergo a series of changes in autumn which enables them to withstand stresses associated with freezing. The approach of winter, with its longer nights and shorter days, signals woody plants to begin a hardening process. The more acclimated plants are to winter, the hardier they are said to be.

Growth stops in woody plants some time before the first frost. A certain number of degree days of chilling temperatures follows the growth stoppage and a rest period begins. Much of the living material in the plants' cells changes to a gel-like state. As a result, very little water remains free inside the cells, so freezing is avoided. The plants then gradually release heat before the actual freezing of certain portions. Hardening results from several separate physical changes. It is an active, gradual process, not just something that happens.

With the return of warmer temperatures, the hardening process is reversed. Because of the temperature's influence on the thawing of ice, the photoperiod has a less dramatic effect on the rejuvenation of plants. For this reason, unseasonably warm temperatures in early spring followed by a frost can damage the hardiest of plants. In most cases, late frost injury affects the younger shoots and buds.

In addition to freezing, desiccation (drying out), abrasion, snow load, and icing are the winter stresses that require adaptations by woody plants.

Winter may appear to be a time when there is much available moisture, but actually the air is often very dry. The snow reflects the sunlight, which evaporates moisture. The ever-present winter winds then carry off the moisture. Much water remains unavailable to plants in the form of frozen snow crystals. How woody plants adapt to the dry conditions differs among leaf-bearing and coniferous or cone-bearing (evergreen) species. During days when the sun is brightly shining, some water is absorbed by conifers. Conifer needles are coated with a waxy substance that helps retain water. Small breathing pores located on the underside of the needles can be kept closed. This further aids conifers in conserving water. Water is replenished during occasional thawing periods.

Growing upright helps many woody plants reduce physical damage from wind-carried ice particles such as sleet and freezing rain. White birch trees can bend under a load of weighty snow. They return to an upright position in spring. The hemlocks, with their broad, spreading branches, also bend under snow and ice. Still, damage is often caused by wet heavy snow and accumulations of ice. If a twig or branch snaps during winter, the plant tissue is torn and dies.

Winter Tree Identification

Most broad-leafed trees in the northeast and north central United States and southern Canada are without leaves for six or more months. Many people are able to identify trees in summer by their leaves, but they wonder how trees can be identified in winter. Bare winter twigs, like the summer leaves, have specific characteristics that are different on each woody plant. You may find identifying twigs in winter difficult at first, but when you become familiar with the various parts, you will be able to identify winter twigs by their buds and bark.

Before using a twig key to identify trees in winter, look

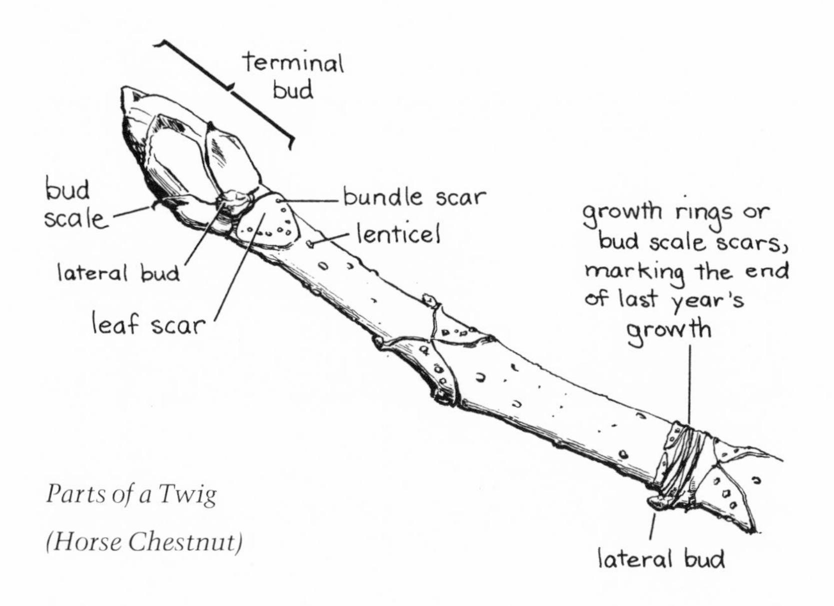

Parts of a Twig

(Horse Chestnut)

at the labeled illustration of a twig. Compare this to an actual twig. Become familiar with the names of the various parts.

The size, shape, and position of each bud is important, as is the texture and the color of the twig and trunk surfaces. Smell and taste the outer and inner bark. Is it sweet or sour? The arrangement of the buds indicates the patterns of the leaves on the tree. The leaf scars are the joints where the old leaves were attached to the twig. Within the scars are tiny dots. These are the bundle scars, which were left by tubes that carried nutrient-containing sap between the twig and the leaf. Lenticels, small pores, form speckled patterns along the twig. Some are large and warty, others are small and smooth, but they all serve the same purpose. Oxygen and other gases flow through them. The buds should be arranged along the twig like one of the following:

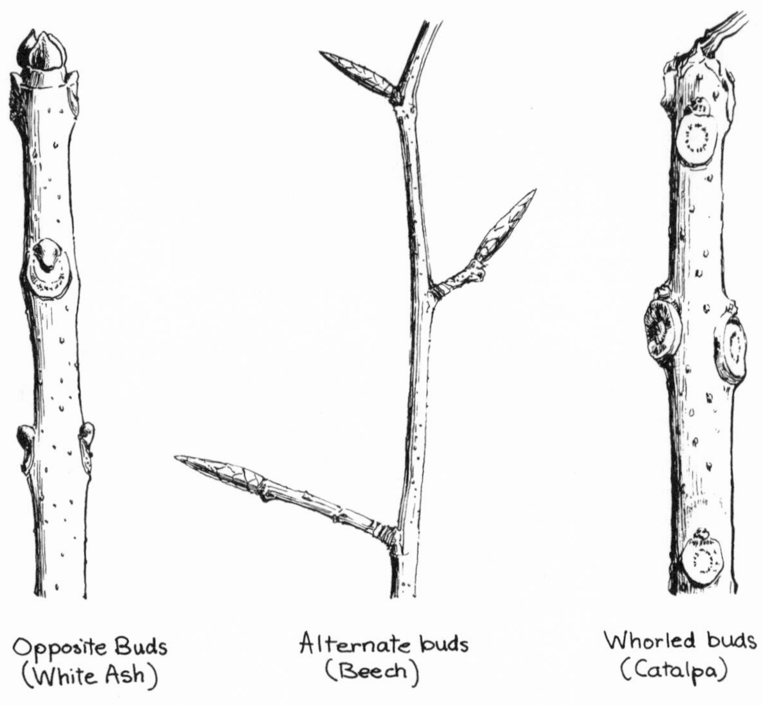

How are the buds arranged on the twig you have been studying?

If you cut the twig crosswise or lengthwise, you will discover a pith located in the center of the stem. The pith in a crosswise cut will resemble one of the following:

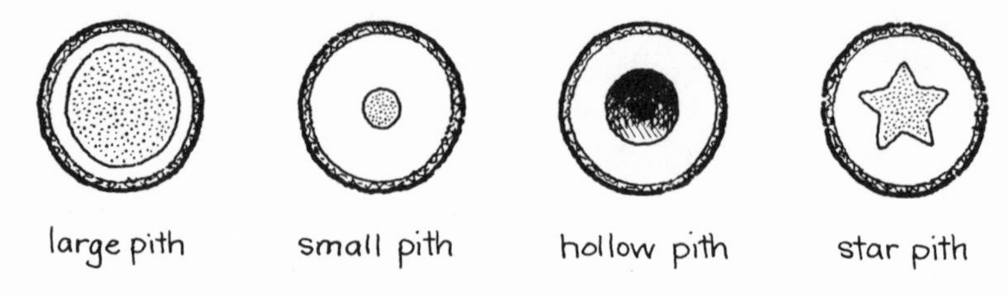

In a lengthwise cut it will look like one of these:

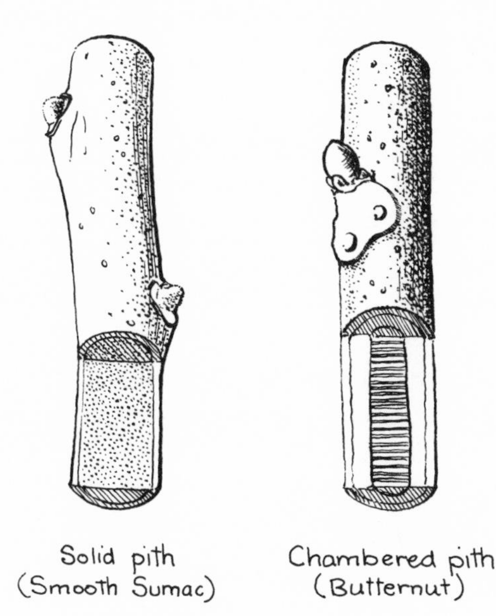

Solid pith (Smooth Sumac) Chambered pith (Butternut)

Cut and collect a number of twigs 4 to 6 inches long. Look for twigs with similar features. Try to group them according to characteristics. Be sure that each twig put into a group shares a particular characteristic with all the other twigs in that group. By doing this you will be able to make your own identification key. Here are some questions that will help you:

1. Are the buds opposite, alternate, or whorled?

2. Are the buds grouped in a bunch at the end of the twig, or is there only one bud at the end of the twig?

3. What color is the twig?

4. How are the bundle scars arranged? What shape are they?

5. Are the buds large or small?

Can you think of any other questions that can help you make an identification key?

On page 145 are listed many trees that commonly can be found in the northeast and north central United States and southern Canada.

Identification keys are available in several sources listed at the end of this book. Your local library should have the sources or be able to obtain them.

Growth Rings

Each spring a tree grows a light-colored ring under its bark. In summer, a dark ring grows. The growth then stops until the following spring. These rings are easily seen when a tree has been sawed down. Locate a cut stump along the road or in the woods near your house or school. Count the rings from the middle of the stump to the outside. The complete year's growth is represented by one light ring and one dark ring. Determine the age of the tree and observe the size of the stump.

Rings will also tell you about the life of the tree. A wide ring indicates there was plenty of water, sunlight, and food that season. An adequate amount of these essentials during that year enabled the tree to grow many new cells. A thin ring shows a lack of water, food, or sunlight. It may have resulted from drought, or from competition among this particular tree and other trees and shrubs. If the tree has been exposed to a fire, the scars will show.

Cones

Search for cones of various evergreen trees as you walk through the woods. Are the cones you find open or closed? Are they on the ground or hanging on the tree? If

you find closed cones, collect some from various trees. Put a group of cones from different trees in a cold place, and another group near a stove or radiator. Can you predict which group will open first? Which species within each group will open first? If some of the cones haven't opened after a week, put them in a 225° oven and dry them for 20 to 25 minutes. When the cones open, take out some seeds, plant them, and see if they grow. Put other seeds from the cones in the bird feeder. Which birds eat them? Do the birds eat only certain kinds of cone seeds?

How do the seeds compare in shape and size? How about the shape and size of the cones? Are they the same or different? Make a collection of cones from the various cone-bearing trees in your neighborhood, displaying both the cones and the seeds.

Tree Shapes

Trees have distinctive shapes. The form of a particular kind of tree can be observed more easily in winter because the lack of leaf cover enables the tree to be silhouetted against the winter sky. Observe the various shapes. Some trees are spreading like the elm and apple; others are erect, like poplars and evergreens. Sketch some that you like. Compare your drawings. Can you see distinct differences among the trees you have sketched? The easiest tree to sketch is one that is growing in an open location where it has been allowed to develop free of competition from others.

When Leaves Don't Fall

Have you ever seen any trees that do not let go of their leaves in winter even though the leaves are obviously dead and have turned brown? In the fall, trees begin to withdraw food materials for winter storage. A corky layer forms between the base of the leaf stem and the twig. Soon the leaf stem breaks at the base and the leaf falls from the tree. In some trees, the corky layer does not form completely and though the leaf dies, it does not fall from the tree. Can you find trees that do not lose their leaves in winter? Which are they?

Does Bark Differ?

Find different kinds of trees within the same area that are approximately the same size. Using a piece of drawing paper and a wax crayon, make rubbings at the same height and on the same side of the trees. Compare the rubbings. What pattern does each make? What differences or similarities can you see?

Again choose a number of trees. Press soft clay against the bark of each so that an imprint of the bark is left on the clay. (Keeping the clay warm and soft on a very cold winter day may be difficult. Try keeping it under your arm or inside your parka. You can warm the clay by placing it near a heater. Then wrap it in newspaper. Can you think of other ways to keep it warm and soft?) Remove the clay from the bark, peeling it off slowly so that the bark print is not damaged. When you get it home, circle the print with a cardboard collar. Pour plaster of Paris, mixed with water and a teaspoon of salt (to speed hardening), into the clay print. (The plaster of Paris should be the consistency of glue or melted ice cream.)

Let the plaster harden for 30 minutes to 1 hour. Then remove the clay carefully. A pattern of bark is left permanently in the plaster. The plaster print may be painted to match the color of the tree bark from which it was printed. What pattern does each make? What differences or similarities can you see?

Try These Activities

Cut open the winter leaf buds, crosswise and lengthwise. Use a magnifying lens to observe how each is stowed away for winter.

Discover the similarities and differences in bud scales. Are some sticky? How does that protect the bud?

Cut a twig and place it in a glass of water inside a warm room. After a time (maybe as long as two or three weeks), the buds will sprout.

Search for fruits and seeds of plants on the snow. Where are the plants they came from? How did they get to where you found them? Look at them under a magnifying lens. How are they similar and different?

Winter Wild Drinks

Even in winter, natural foods are available. Below are some recipes for hot and cold drinks from the wild. When you make these drinks, be sure to use only the specified plants. Don't experiment with other plants, as this could be dangerous to your health.

Birch Tea:

The twigs of yellow, black, or white birch can be used, but yellow and black are best. Collect a bunch of young twigs and break them into small pieces to fit into a pot. Add water and bring it to a boil. Let the mixture boil for

10 to 15 minutes, until the water has turned dark. Strain the tea and add honey or drink it plain.

WINTERGREEN TEA:

Wintergreen is a low-growing plant, so it may be difficult to find when there is heavy snow cover. To make the tea, collect a handful of leaves and steep them in boiling water. Add honey or drink it plain. Wintergreen berries improve in taste with freezing, but they can be eaten raw.

LABRADOR TEA:

Labrador tea is the name of a plant. It is usually found in cold mountain bogs and forests. When crushed, the flowers produce a fragrant aroma. The leaves are used for making tea. Dry them completely in the sun, in front of a fire, or in a low oven. Prepare the tea by steeping the leaves in boiling water. It is good served hot or cold.

SUMAC LEMONADE:

The fruit of the sumac is covered with hairs that are rich in malic acid. Malic acid is found in apples and can be extracted from the sumac fruit to make a cold drink similar to lemonade. After the first frost is the best time to collect the ripe fruit, which is a crimson-brown color. Bruise the berries lightly by rubbing the clump through your hands. Soak the berries in cold water until the water turns pinkish. Pour the mixture through cheesecloth or a fine strainer, add honey to taste, chill, and serve.

Maple Sugaring

Sap will flow anytime from fall well into spring, each time a period of below-freezing temperature is followed by a period of warmer weather. In late February and into March, temperatures range from 25°F at night up to 40°F to 50°F during the daytime. These are ideal conditions for sap flow.

Most species of maple and birch produce sap that can be used to make syrup. They have varying degrees of sweetness. Sugar maple and a similar species, black maple, are primarily used for commercial production. Sap usually flows first from the south side of the tree, because of its exposure to the sun, but this makes no real difference in the overall amount of sap obtained from a tree during a sugaring season. Production of northern- and southern-sided taps is about the same.

There may be producers of maple syrup near where you live. Check with them to see whether they might allow you and a group of friends or family members to visit during sugaring season.

If you would like to try making a small amount of syrup yourself, you will need some equipment, most of which can be improvised. Be certain to get permission from the people who own the trees before you begin tapping. Also, be aware that you will not obtain much syrup for your efforts. It takes between 20 and 40 gallons of sap to make 1 gallon of syrup.

The spout, or spile, allows the sap to flow from the hole to the collecting container and keeps bacteria from getting into the moist hole. Spiles can be made from black elderberry or staghorn sumac twigs. They should be no larger than ¾ inch in diameter and 5 to 6 inches long. Cut a twig to the desired length and remove the pith. The pith in these plants is soft and easily removed by pushing a twig or wire from one end through to the other, leaving a hollow tube. Plastic or metal spiles are used by commercial producers and can be purchased at your local hardware or feed store.

The hole should be drilled into the tree 2 to 2½ inches deep at a slight upward angle. The wood will appear to be wet when you reach the sapwood. The hole should be drilled at a height of about 4 to 5 feet. This will make it easier to work with when the collecting bucket is full. Use a 3/8-inch or 7/16-inch wood bit. Insert the spile about 1½ inches into the hole. Two spiles can be used on a tree 17 to 20 inches in diameter and four spiles can be used on a tree 30 inches in diameter.

A container should be chosen that will be easy to carry when full. (To choose a bucket, fill several with water and try carrying them for a while.) The container can be metal, wooden, or plastic but it should be kept covered, to keep out moisture and insects, and attached to the spile to catch the sap.

The collected sap must be boiled down to evaporate the water and thicken the liquid. Stir it occasionally to prevent the sap from burning. A large flat pan or kettle kept over a fire will work quite well. Do not boil the sap down in the house. The evaporating water will collect on the walls and make a mess. A small camping stove can be used outside. Have an adult help with this.

Once the syrup reaches the consistency of olive oil, it can be left to cool and then put into containers. It will take approximately two hours to reach this thickness.

The sap can also be boiled until a thickness similar to molasses is reached. Pour it in long thin strips onto clean packed snow, and you will have a chewy candy.

About ten to twelve gallons of sap can be obtained from a single tap hole, although there have been trees that have produced 60 gallons from a tap hole in a single season. If you have tapped the tree properly, it will not be seriously injured. The hole made by a 7/16-inch bit will heal in two to three years. One made with a larger bit takes much longer to heal. Do not use the same spile holes for two consecutive years.

5. Searching for Small Creatures: Insects and Galls

When cold weather arrives, temperatures fall, soil freezes, trees lose their leaves, flowers die, many birds migrate, and ice covers the pond. Where have the insects and other small creatures gone? Do they migrate, like many birds, or hibernate, like woodchucks and frogs? Have they all died?

This chapter includes information about small creatures you are likely to find during your winter searches in both woody areas and water communities. It also introduces you to the structures called galls, which are growths or swellings on the stem of a plant. Formed by insects, mites, fungi, or bacteria, they represent a unique plant-animal relationship.

Insects

For purposes of classification, the plant and animal kingdoms are divided into six categories, which are (in descending order): phylum, class, order, family, genus, and species. In the animal kingdom, those without backbones, invertebrates (phylum *Arthropoda*), constitute 80 percent of all living creatures. All arthropods, at some point in their development, have three body divisions (head, thorax, and abdomen), jointed legs (limbs), and an outside skin, or exoskeleton, made of a very hard material. This exoskeleton must be shed at various times during the arthropod's life, allowing it to grow. There are many classes in this phylum. For example, members of the class *Arachnida* (including spiders, ticks, scorpions, and mites) have more than three pairs of legs, no apparent antennae, and no wings. Members of the class *Crustacea* (such as crayfish, barnacles, and crabs) have two pairs of antennae, at least five pairs of legs, and no wings. Each organism has certain characteristics that determine the class to which it belongs.

A full-grown insect (class *Insecta*) has three distinct parts to its body: the head, the thorax (the middle part to which are attached the legs and wings), and the abdomen (the hindmost part). It also has a pair of "feelers" (antennae), which project from the head; three pairs of jointed legs; and usually two pairs of wings.

Insect Life Cycles

Each species of insect has a specific life cycle. Knowing how insects grow and develop will help you to recognize insect forms. The three basic life cycles are described below.

The Four-Stage Life Cycle

The small creatures start as *eggs* deposited by an adult female, in most species from an ovipositer, or egg depositer, that is located at the tip of the abdomen. The eggs hatch into a wormlike form called *larva*. At this point the small creature has a distinctly different appearance from the adult and it feeds most of the time. The larva makes a *pupa* case, or cocoon, inside which it develops wings and reproductive organs; it also forms new mouth parts and the antennae and legs grow. Eventually the small creature emerges from the pupa as a full-grown *adult*, ready to reproduce. The adults lay eggs and start the life cycle once more. Butterflies and moths develop in this way.

The Three-Stage Life Cycle

The small creatures begin as *eggs* deposited by an adult. The hatched eggs are called *nymphs*. Some of them resemble the adult form except they have no wings and their head is larger than their body. Other nymphs feed continuously and go through a series of molts, or shedding of the outer skin. The nymph resembles its parent more and more with each molt. In the final molt it emerges with wings and it is an *adult*, capable of laying eggs. Stoneflies and dragonflies develop in this way.

The Series-of-Molts Life Cycle

There is a group of insects, made up of a number of species, that hatch from the egg as an exact copy of their parent except for the size. They go through a series of molts until they reach a final form. In the final stage they are mature and capable of reproduction. The number of molts differs from species to species. Springtails and bristletails are examples of this kind of development.

How Insects Spend the Winter

Some species of small creatures winter as adult forms, while others winter as eggs and larvae. The eggs and larvae will emerge in spring as adults to carry on the species. Some insects hibernate, a few even migrate, and others that are parasites live on as they do in other seasons. There is also a group of true winter insects that are active throughout the winter months. You should be able to find all the forms in your search — adult, egg, and larva. Insects are cold-blooded. Their temperature is not controlled internally like mammals'. Insects' temperature changes with the temperature of the air. Cold slows down their movements and freezing temperatures can kill them very quickly.

Insects are more diverse than mammals in their approach to surviving winter conditions. Hibernation doesn't quite describe overwintering in an egg or pupa. The term *diapause* is used to describe what occurs in insects. Diapause involves a stop in growth and reduced rates of body processes — breathing, heart beat, and temperature. It may occur long before the start of adverse conditions and continue for months after good conditions have returned. Under normal conditions, for instance, it only takes an insect egg a few days to hatch. There are some eggs that start development, then stop and go into a quiet stage that may last all summer and winter. Growth does not begin again until the conditions are right in spring.

There are also insects that avoid the stresses of winter by migrating. The monarch butterfly is the best known. In the fall this orange, brown, and black insect leaves the northeast and north central United States and southern Canada on a long journey southward. Monarchs begin life as caterpillars on the milkweed plant, changing to adults in time to group with others. It is known that they winter in Florida and Mexico, but how they migrate, or which route they take, is yet a mystery. Even less is known about the journey to warmer climates by the painted lady butterfly. Some migrate, while others winter over in sheltered spots in dead logs, hollow trees, and buildings. Some buckeyes migrate along the Atlantic coast beaches, while others hibernate. There are little sulfurs that travel over the open ocean to Bermuda, while others hibernate as pupae.

Because insects are cold-blooded, they must winter in a frost-free place if they do not hibernate. Most of those insects that migrate do not travel long distances south. The long southward journey is reserved for a select few species. The majority of insects migrate downward. Japanese beetles and May or June beetles migrate to just below the frost line. Earthworms travel downward as deep as 6 feet. When you go outside on a cold day in January, with three feet of snow accumulation, stop for a minute and think about all the insects that are right below your feet—under the snow, under the grass, below the frozen soil, deep in the earth.

Searching for Small Creatures on Land

If you wish to go on a small-creature search in or near your house or in the woods, there are many places to look. Here are a few likely places: under shingles or loose bark; behind shutters; in cracks around windows; in cellars, barns, garages, and covered bridges; in hollow trees, rotting logs, bark crevices, piles of leaves, clumps of grass, and galls. Can you add to this list? Which of these and other places has the most small creatures? How do the temperatures in the locations compare? Are they similar? Different? Are they colder than the open-air temperature? Remember that every winter home should provide protection from the weather and safety from predators. Insect-eating birds that have not migrated south will be searching for small creatures to feed on. Watch the woodpeckers, nuthatches, chickadees, and tufted titmice. Where do they find food? Can you locate any small creatures by probing in the same nooks?

Equipment

If you just plan to look for small creatures, the only equipment you will really need is a small flashlight and a thermometer. The flashlight will enable you to explore dark corners and hidden places, indoors and out. The thermometer will be useful in locating places where the temperature is warmer, even on a cold day. Remember, most small creatures hide in sites that are dark and protected from the wind and cold.

If you plan to collect small creatures as well as observe them, bring along the following items: small plastic bags, a small vial or plastic jar, a small pocket knife, straight pins, tweezers, and a hand magnifying lens.

True Winter Insects

There exists a group of insects that you may discover crawling over the surface of the snow or emerging from a crack. These insects, which spend at least part of the winter out and about, are considered the true winter insects. Their life cycles are interesting and varied.

Winter Stonefly. In the latter part of January and early February, the winter stonefly nymph emerges from its water habitat. Its last nymphal skin has become tight. Once the insect reaches the bank of the pond, its nymphal skin splits down the back and the adult emerges. It feeds on algae found on trees and other plants. Males and females then mate. When mating has been

Stonefly

Field Journals

An excellent way to keep track of the small creatures — eggs, larvae, pupae, or adults — you locate is to begin a journal or a record-card collection. The information will be helpful when returning the insect to the place where it was found and also will provide a record of particular abundances of small creatures. If you ever want to show someone a certain insect form, or you want to search again, the information recorded will be useful. Your notes of observations can be added to as the insect forms change, develop, and emerge in spring. Below is a sample information card.

Kind of small creature ____________________
Stage of development
(egg, larva, pupa, adult) ____________________
Where found ____________________
Date ____________________
Observations of behavior ____________________
What was it doing? ____________________
Was it alone or with others (same species or different)? ____________________
Other observations ____________________

completed, the females crawl or fly back to the water to lay their eggs. Larger varieties of stoneflies emerge in late February or early March. These varieties feed on the buds of trees.

The winter stonefly is less than ½ inch long and is dark gray in color. It has chewing mouth parts that enable it to feed on algae and tree buds. The stonefly has two slender antennae and two tails attached to the abdomen.

If you find a stonefly while exploring in winter, pick it up and carefully observe it. Use a hand magnifying glass to examine it closely. Is it a nymph or an adult? Can you observe the mouth parts? Can you locate any nymphal skins (shucks) left behind? Where would be the best place to look for the discarded skins?

Springtails. Springtails, or snow fleas, are the most common true winter insects found by investigators.

Insect Models

Make models of the winter insects you find. Try to duplicate their delicate parts. Here are some suggestions for materials to construct insect models:

Body: Empty egg cartons, milk cartons, papier-mâché around a balloon

Legs: Popsicle sticks, pipe cleaners, small twigs

Head: Acorns, acorn caps, hickory nuts, walnuts, cattail heads, bottle caps

Many materials — such as containers and other items normally thrown away — can be used. Construct models of different sizes: life size, giant, or exactly to scale. Color detailed features by using felt-tip markers or paint.

They are particularly abundant on days in late winter when the temperature rises above freezing. Springtails are the oldest known fossil insects. Fossils 300 million years old have been discovered in Scotland. They have also been found in amber (tree sap hardened millions of years ago) in Canada. Springtails follow the series-of-molts life cycle; they have no wings. They travel by means of a tail that contains two spines. This tail is folded forward on the underside of the abdomen and held in place by a latch-type organ. The tail is released and is forced down against the ground, propelling the insect in a springing manner. Because springtails are very small (most are less than 6 millimeters long), they are rarely seen, except on sunny days in mid- to late winter when they appear to flock in large numbers to the snow surface. Masses of these tiny insects can be seen in snowshoe tracks or footprints. They feed on decaying vegetation, sap, algae, and fungi spores. The best place to locate springtails is at the base of a decaying tree that has fungus growing from its trunk and branches. When you locate a group of springtails, observe their behavior for a short time. Look closely at their body structure, using a hand magnifying lens. Place one or more in a plastic container with sides at least 1 inch high and observe how the insect travels. Locate its tail and watch it move.

Winter Crane Fly. The winter crane fly looks like a very large mosquito with long slender legs. The crane fly emerges from the snow to mate. The female returns immediately under the snow and lays her eggs in dead leaves and other decaying matter that covers the ground. The crane flies walk on the snow because they have no true wings at this stage of development. Their mouth parts are designed for sucking. They do not bite. If you are lucky enough to see one in late winter, look closely at its

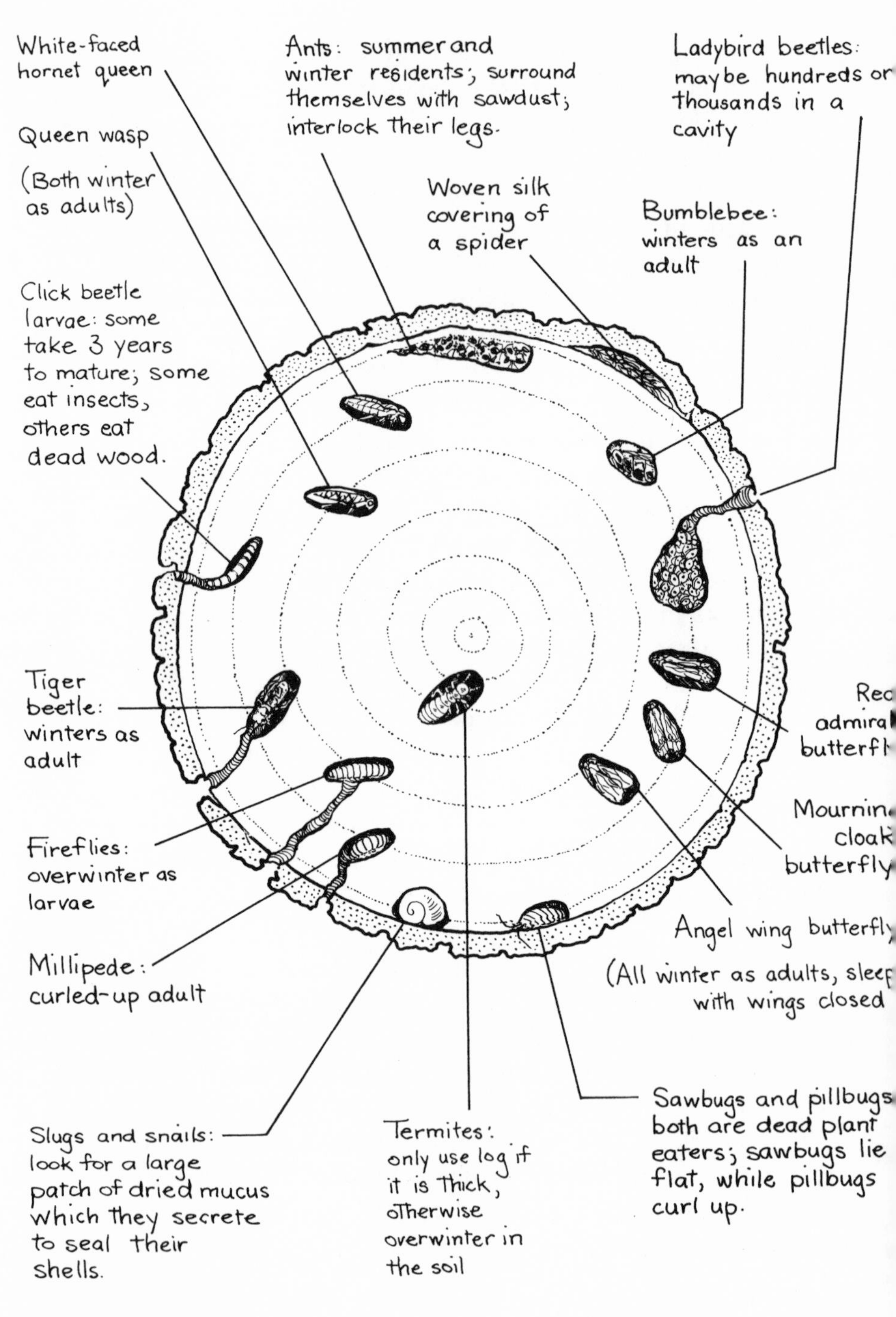

White-faced hornet queen
Ants: summer and winter residents; surround themselves with sawdust; interlock their legs.
Ladybird beetles: maybe hundreds or thousands in a cavity
Queen wasp
(Both winter as adults)
Woven silk covering of a spider
Bumblebee: winters as an adult
Click beetle larvae: some take 3 years to mature; some eat insects, others eat dead wood.
Tiger beetle: winters as adult
Fireflies: overwinter as larvae
Millipede: curled-up adult
cloak
butterfly
Angel wing
(All winter as adults,
with wings closed
Slugs and snails: look for a large patch of dried mucus which they secrete to seal their shells.
Termites: only use log if it is thick, otherwise overwinter in the soil
Sawbugs and pillbugs both are dead plant eaters; sawbugs lie flat, while pillbugs curl up.

A Decaying Log

During the summer months, numerous insects live in a decaying log. Termites are one example. When winter comes, they leave their log home and migrate into the soil. Many other insects who live near but outside the log during the summer inhabit the hollowed spaces left vacant by the departed summer residents. Some of the many winter log inhabitants are illustrated here, in the locations where they would most likely be found.

What kind of small creature can you find in a decaying log? Where did you find it? Under the bark? In a burrow? In the wood itself? Can you identify the kind of log? Lift rotting logs and see what you can find beneath. Try to return the log to the position in which you found it.

mouth parts, using a hand magnifying lens. How does the structure of the mouth differ from the chewing parts of the winter stonefly? Are the body parts similar to or different from the other winter insects you have found? Make a sketch of each and compare.

Winter Scorpionfly. The winter scorpionfly emerges from the snow, and from decaying logs that are covered with moss, from November to March. It has a long beak-type nose that comes to a point; the nose contains the mouth parts. The males have a pair of claspers on the rear of the abdomen. These are used for mating. The females never develop wings, while the males have an imperfectly formed pair and rarely fly.

How do these true winter insects compare in size? When you find one, measure its length, using any flat surface that is straight (such as a Popsicle stick). Mark the length, using a letter to indicate the species, and the date. Compare this measurement to measurements of other winter insects of the same and different species. Does the length differ according to when you find the insects?

Collecting

Find a variety of small creatures, bring them inside, and identify them. Observe their form and behavior closely outside and then again after bringing them in. When you have finished, return them to the place they were found.

You may wish to find out what happens on a day-to-day basis. It is interesting to observe the development during winter and see the emergence in spring. This can be done by keeping the various insect forms you have collected in a container outside until spring. Make periodic observations and record them. Caution should be taken not to keep the insect forms inside for a long period of time during the winter. This will create a false spring and may affect their normal changes.

The best type of container for the insects is one made of clear plastic or fine wire mesh, which allows you to see what is happening and prevents the insect from escaping. If you use a solid chamber, be certain to make air holes. The holes must be very small and should be covered with gauze so that air can flow freely but the insect cannot escape.

A terrarium such as the one on page 85 creates a very comfortable habitat for the emerging small creatures.

Empty oatmeal boxes and old nylon stockings can be

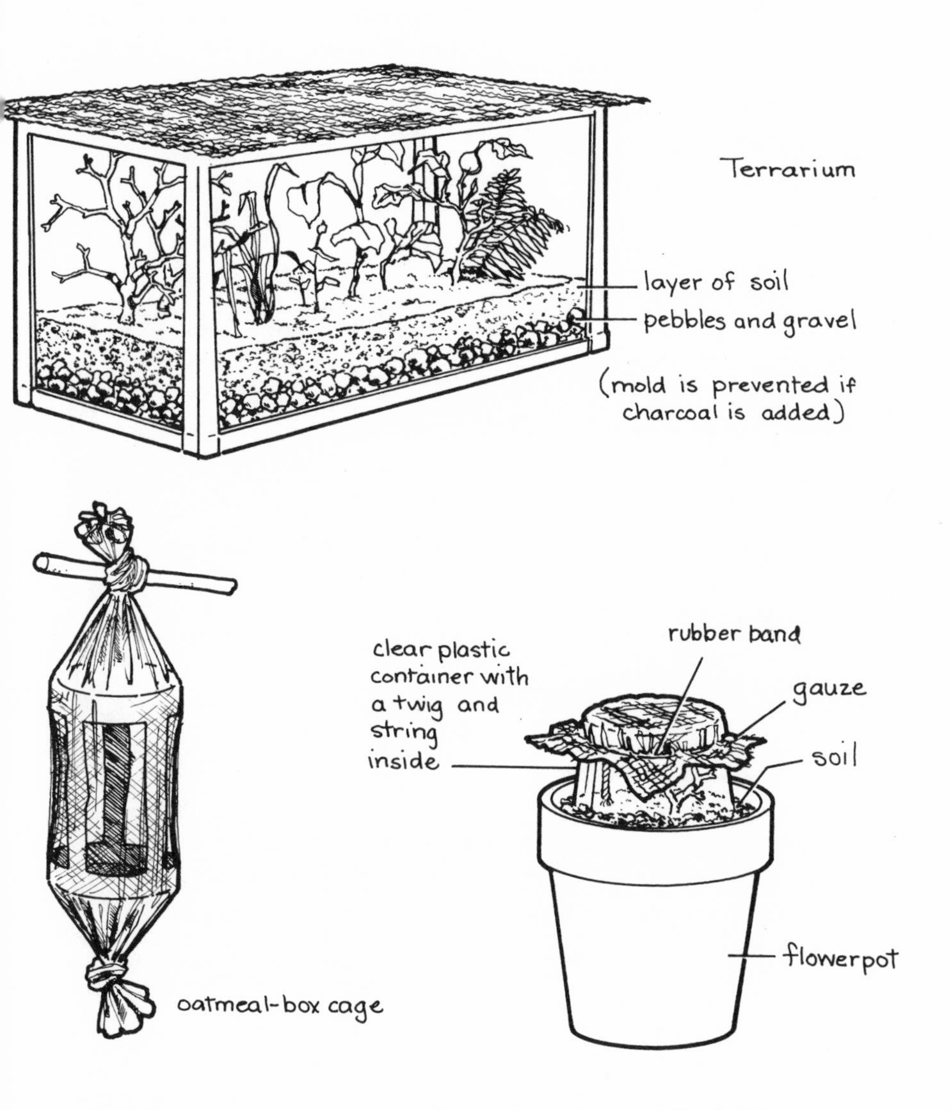

used to make cages. Cut the feet from the stockings and tie a knot in the bottom. Place the box, which has been cut as shown in the accompanying drawing, inside the stocking. Put the insects you wish to keep in the box, and tie a knot in the top to close it. The cage can then be hung outside.

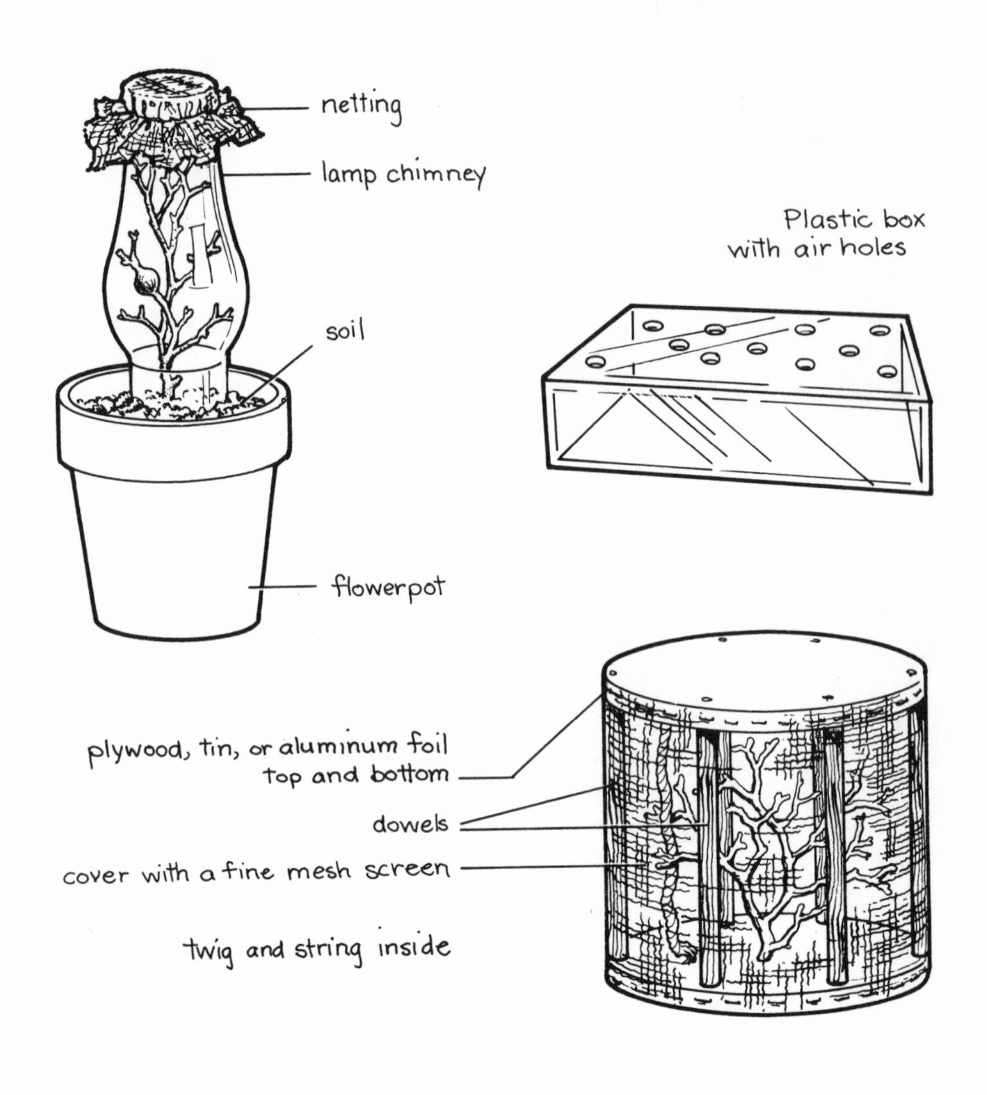

Small creatures collected inside the house should be kept inside for observation. The idea is to try to duplicate the conditions of the winter home from which they were taken. House crickets and field crickets are two good examples of creatures commonly found indoors during winter. They will eat meat, vegetables, bread, and small seeds. Experiment to determine which food they prefer. Crickets often will kill each other, so keep them in separate cages. Use your imagination to create their houses. Be sure to provide their basic needs: food, water, and shelter. Observe the behavior of the caged crickets and make a record of what you observe. Pay attention to details. How do they move and feed? Where do they spend most of their time, in a sheltered place or in the light? If you have two or more caged crickets, look for similarities and differences in form and behavior.

Cocoons can be found attached to trees, weeds, and shrubs in fields during winter. They become exposed after the leaves drop in the fall. If cocoons are collected before the first good frost and not exposed to the cold, they will not hatch until April. If the cocoons are gathered after they have been out in three or four weeks of winter weather, they will hatch about four weeks after being brought inside.

Be sure to keep a record of where and when they were collected. Record the kind of plant to which each cocoon was attached, if you can identify it.

After collecting the cocoons, keep them in an open shoe box. Keep them moist by sprinkling with water at least once a week, and turn them at the same time. As the insect inside gets ready to emerge, the cocoon will stretch some. It is a good idea to cover the box in late March with a fine wire-mesh screen or cheesecloth. The emerging creature may be a flying one. What kind of creature emerged from your cocoon?

Egg cases of the praying mantis can also be found in the fall and early winter. They may be attached to grass, weeds, shrubs, and small trees. The mantis cases, usually attached to the entire twig, are brownish beige and have the texture of hard cotton candy. Treat the cases as you did the cocoons, except cover them within one month after bringing them inside. From 50 to 200 will hatch from one case. These can be kept and fed raw hamburger. They often eat each other, so don't be alarmed when this occurs. Release them in the spring when the other insects come out. Praying mantises are very helpful, as they consume many insects.

Small-Creature Strainer

Many insects spend the winter embedded in plant material, where they are protected from the cold and from predators. How can we get these small creatures to come out and show themselves? One way to accomplish this is by using a small-creature strainer. To make one you will need a quart-sized jar, some rubbing alcohol, a wide-mouthed funnel (or improvise one, using aluminum foil), a small piece of wire screening, and a lamp with a 75 or 100 watt light bulb.

Collect from under the snow: dead leaves and plant material, shredded and rotten wood, birds' nests, plant material from inside a tree hole, and any other plant material that you think would make a good winter home for small creatures. Put the materials into separate plastic bags and label each bag so that you know where the material was gathered. When you return home with the materials, leave them outside until you are ready to use them.

Pour approximately 1 inch of rubbing alcohol into the jar. This will act as a preservative. (If you prefer not to kill the insects, use water instead.) Stand the funnel in the jar and place the screening in the funnel. Put a handful of the collected materials into the funnel, resting on the screen. Set the jar under the lamp so that the heat of the light will dry out the funnel's contents. As the material inside the funnel dries, the small creatures will begin

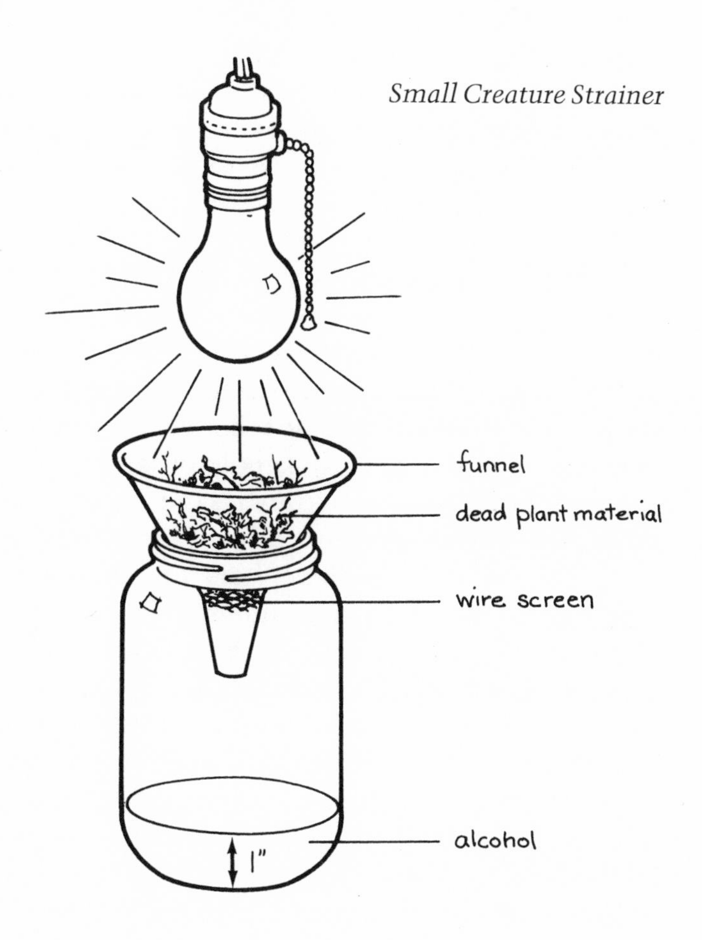

to thaw out and move down lower to avoid the heat and keep from drying out. The small creatures will continue to move until they drop into the alcohol at the bottom of the jar, where they will be preserved. Four to six hours should be long enough to drive out all the small creatures that were inhabiting the material. Pour the alcohol through a piece of paper towel or filter paper. Use a hand magnifying lens to observe any small creature that you have collected.

A simpler method of separating the insects from the plant material is to put a small portion of one sample into an aluminum pie plate, a flame-proof dish, or a piece of aluminum foil with the edges curled up. Place the container on top of the stove and turn the burner on to low. Observe the sample and try to identify the insect or other small creature that emerges. How is it structured? Does it have wings? How many legs does it have? In what stage of development is it? Place the small creatures in individual vials, small boxes, or other containers. Keep the small creatures from each sample of material separate. Repeat this process using other samples. Do the same small creatures emerge from different materials? In what area of the woods or back yard did you find the greatest number of small creatures hidden? In soil or leaves? Which area produced the greatest variety of species? Keeping records will be of great help if you want to make sense of your findings. Jot down the information that you discovered during this activity. The form presented earlier in this chapter can be used for record keeping.

Grouping

If you become very interested in insects you may want to group them by their properties and try to determine relationships. Grouping the insects by their characteristics is a means of identifying. Look for characteristics or specific parts or structures that are very similar. Ask yourself questions about the insects you are trying to group. For example: Do they have backbones? How many main body parts do they have? Do they have wings? How many legs do they have? How many antennae? Are their mouth parts sucking or biting parts?

Searching for Small Creatures in Water Communities

Water insects, as well as land insects, must be adapted in order to survive winter's low temperatures and the scarcity of food. They must have an inactive, resistant, or protected stage that normally occurs during winter. This stage may be any of the four life stages — egg, larva, pupa, adult. The following partial list represents the forms of each insect you will find during a winter water search.

Insects that pass the winter as adults. Backswimmers, water boatmen, small giant water bugs, large giant water bugs, and whirligig beetles burrow into the mud in the bottom of streams and ponds. Water scavenger beetles and diving beetles burrow in the mud of the bottom or banks and in the sides of pools. Marsh treaders hibernate under the rubbish along the banks. Waterscorpions burrow into the mud of a sheltered bank. Mosquitos hibernate under boards, trash, and rubbish, although they may also pass the winter as larvae and are sometimes found frozen in the ice but become active when thawed out. Water striders pass the winter in the mud, under leaves or rubbish on the banks, or at the bottom of pools.

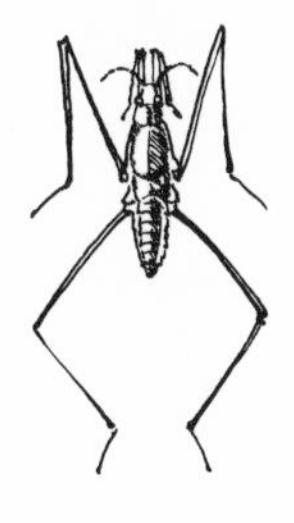
Water strider

Insects that pass the winter in the pupal stage. Of the common water insects, only some mayflies pass the winter in this stage.

Insects that pass the winter as larvae or nymphs. Damselflies, dragonflies, bloodworms, and dobsonflies pass the winter in this stage in the bottoms of streams and pools, as do some mayflies and some stoneflies. Some stoneflies emerge in the winter and have been found transforming on the edge of the ice. As stated above, mosquitos have been found in the larval stage in midwinter.

Winter Collecting

As we have seen, many common water insects pass the winter as adults or larvae. Anyone who knows something about the winter hiding places of water insects and who has the ambition and energy will usually find his collecting efforts rewarded. Collecting requires close observation, since at this season the insects are more or less immobile and may escape the eye. Small creatures can be found under the ice, among grass or plants, in the mud, in dead and decaying vegetable materials on the bottom, in the air pocket between ice and water, or swimming freely in the water. The choice of habitat is the result of food supply and oxygen needs of the specific small creature. The following general instructions should be helpful if you are a beginner.

1. Turn over and carefully examine masses of leaves, twigs, roots, driftwood, and other rubbish along shores and banks. This kind of collecting can best be carried on when there is no snow on the ground.

2. With a strong dip net or scoop, make sweepings along the surface of the bottom. Dragonfly larvae are often secured in this way, since they are frequently found moving sluggishly along the bottom even in midwinter.

3. Dig into the bottom with the net or scoop and bring up loads of the mud and debris. Wash out each haul thoroughly by scooping up the clear water with the net and letting it drain through. Doing this is very helpful in examining the catch. After this is done, the mass remaining in the net must be examined with considerable care, since such forms as the small giant water bug, large giant water bug, and whirligig beetle come up so torpid and

with so complete a coating of mud that they are often indiscernible.

4. Dig into the protected banks, near or slightly above the edge of the water, and follow the instructions given in step 3.

Getting Ready

Be sure to wear warm clothes. This is particularly important when investigating waterways. Ponds, lakes, and marshes are exposed, and the wind in these open areas can produce a colder temperature than in the forest. In addition to the clothing described at the beginning of this book, rubber gloves should be worn for winter water wandering. Wear them over your winter gloves. This will enable you to put your hands in water even on the coldest of days.

You will need a few pieces of equipment for observing and collecting winter water insects: a wide-mouthed quart jar with a top, a pair of tweezers, an eyedropper, a hand magnifying lens, a pan or flat dish, and a dip net or scoop. The scoop can be improvised by tying a kitchen strainer to a pole or broom handle, or by attaching to the pole a metal clothes hanger that has been shaped into a loop and covered with an old nylon stocking or cheesecloth.

Consideration should be given to safety. Take precautions when investigating in winter water habitats. Be absolutely sure the ice is solid before venturing out onto a frozen body of water. Always go with a friend or two. Carry a safety line or a long pole and be certain to tell someone where you are going.

Many of the insects collected in this way are quite sluggish but show movement when disturbed. None are likely to be found in an active state. Most of the inactive specimens liven up when brought into a warm temperature and in time become quite active.

The key on page 147 is intended to provide the collector with a simple means of identifying the common insects of ponds and streams.

If you plan to search for small creatures in a solidly frozen pond, use a metal pole or auger to make a hole in the ice. The hole should be large enough to fit your scoop, but not much larger. If there are any people ice fishing, they may have an auger. Ask them to drill you a hole somewhere near the edge. If the ice is very thin or not frozen solidly enough to be safe, stand on the edge and collect samples with a long-handled scoop.

Once the hole has been made, look into the water. What do you see? If there is a glare from the sun, make a tent over your head with your jacket. This will cut the glare and enable you to see through the surface.

Stick the scoop into the hole and allow it to hit the bottom. Pull the scoop along the bottom so that dead leaves, mud, and other materials are collected. Bring it to the surface and spread its contents on the pan or flat dish. Look for small creatures. Examine them with a hand lens.

A stream is different from a pond because the water is constantly moving. As a result of this movement, many stream insects and other creatures hibernate in the mud, stay near the bank, or find homes under rocks or logs. Look in these places when searching in the winter stream.

A glass or clear plastic bowl or dish can be used to give you a better view in fast-moving streams. Place it on the

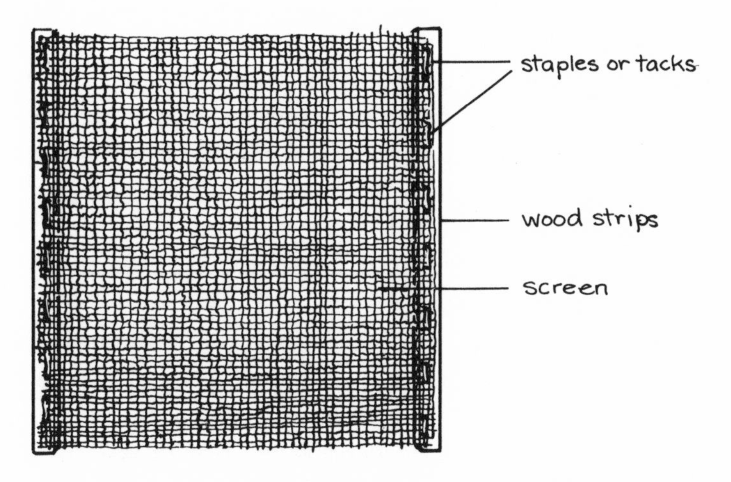

Collecting Screen

surface of the stream and push down. This will enable you to see the bottom more clearly.

A collecting screen can be very useful and is easy to make. All you need is a piece of window screen about 2 feet by 2 feet, two strips of wood (3/8 inch thick, about 1 inch wide, and 2 feet long), and staples or tacks. Staple or tack the screen to the wood as shown in the illustration.

Stand the screen on the stream bottom while someone else stirs up the bottom a few feet upstream. Many small creatures can be collected using this method. Try it. Draw sketches of the ones you find. Do they resemble any you found in the pond during the winter or in any other season? Look closely at any creatures you collect. Inspect them with a hand magnifying lens. Do they have six legs? Are they eggs, nymphs, larvae, or adults? What are the mouth parts like; are they for chewing or sucking?

Pick up rocks in the stream. Turn them over. Look carefully with a hand magnifying lens if you see nothing immediately. Eggs are sometimes translucent and not at all easily noticed. It is important to focus closely if you wish to find all the creatures that inhabit these small places. Remember, they can be found on the underside of rocks, crawling on the bottom, in the mud, and swimming freely. A favorite hiding spot is near the bank in mud or attached to plants, where they are able to avoid being swept downstream.

Keep the collected small creatures in a jar after observing them in the flat dish for as long as the cold permits. Cover the jar before transporting the creatures home for more thorough observation and investigation. Many animals collected from a stream need water with a high oxygen content. They will not survive in an aquarium without a pump and aerator. Some are carnivorous; that is, they will eat other creatures. Be sure to keep them separate.

Some Common Pond and Stream Insects

Following are some of the insects you may encounter in a winter water search. These are but a few of the common forms. They have been selected because of their size, wide distribution, and abundance. Remember, they may be in nonadult stages — eggs, larvae, or nymphs.

Marsh Treaders. These insects are usually overlooked, since they are only about half an inch long, dull dirty brown in color, and quiet in their habits. They are found in other seasons on the surface of the water or on the soft mud of the shoreline where there are plenty of water plants growing. They seem to prefer swamps and stagnant pools and feed on insects that fall into the water.

Whirligig Beetles. During other seasons these oval, blackish, surface beetles can be seen on ponds or sheltered nooks of quiet streams. They always occur in groups,

Jar Aquarium

Collect a jar of water from a pond, lake, or stream. It should contain some creatures you will only see by using a magnifying lens. Add some mud, dead leaves, and a few strands of dead weeds or grass from the edge of the water. Take the jar home and leave it on a windowsill where the sunlight is not bright. Inspect the jar each day for three weeks, examining a drop of water under a magnifying lens. What do you see? What changes do you observe? Does the water get clearer or cloudier? Does the color of the water change? What remains the same?

Compare samples from a gently flowing and rapidly flowing stream; from an unfrozen pond and a solidly frozen pond, or a marsh. What differences do you find? What similarities? Label each sample with the date, place, and description. Try to identify what appears. Draw the creatures. Observe their activity. Do the creatures hurry or stay in one area somewhat inactive? Develop an explanation for what you observed throughout the three weeks.

which may be small or large. Sometimes the group will number about ten, but at other times there will be several thousand. Watch the behavior of one of these groups in its native haunt. The insect's front legs are much longer than its others and are used for grasping food.

Large giant water bug

Large Giant Water Bug. The large giant water bug is the largest of all the water bugs. It is about 2¾ inches long and about 1¼ inches wide, with a broad flattened body. The second and third pairs of legs are heavy, flattened, and oarlike, while the first pair of legs is held forward in a grasping position. The wings lie flat on the back when not in use. The large size alone will enable you to recognize this insect. In other seasons it rests or swims about at the bottom of the pond.

Small Giant Water Bug. This insect, like the large giant water bug, has a broad flat body with two swimming legs and one pair of grasping legs, well-developed wings, and a strong beak. It is much smaller, being a little less than an inch long, and the body is more oval. Muddy ponds containing an abundance of water plants and sluggish streams having a muddy bottom are its common habitats. During other seasons the small giant water bug comes to the surface frequently to get a supply of air. It feeds on many water insects and larvae, such as water boatmen, backswimmers, dragonfly and mayfly nymphs, and sometimes its own young. It also attacks snails and young fish.

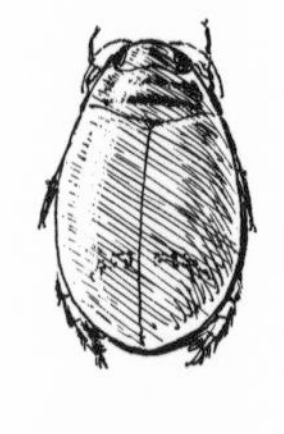
Predaceous diving beetle

Predaceous Diving Beetles. Both the adult beetles and their larvae can be found at other seasons in almost any weedy pool of stagnant or standing water. These beetles and their larvae are the most bloodthirsty of all the water beetles. They are a terror to the smaller water insects as well as to young fish and tadpoles. In fact, the larvae are more fierce than the adults, and are constantly feeding on almost every living form they can capture. These insects often hide in the partly submerged vegetation near the shore. Handle the larvae carefully, as they are easily killed. Do not put larvae and adults into the same jar.

Water Scavenger Beetles. These large, oval, blackish beetles may be found in the same streams and ponds as the predaceous diving beetles. At first sight they resemble the diving beetles, but they differ from them in having no yellow on the body, in hanging with the head instead of the tip of the abdomen at the surface of the water, and in moving the swimming legs alternately instead of at the same time. They feed largely on plants and decaying matter.

Backswimmer. One may expect to find the backswimmer in any pool or stream that contains vegetation. It can be recognized in the water by the fact that it always swims upside-down. The back is shaped like the bottom of a boat, and the flattened hind legs, which are much longer than the others, act as oars. The colors are usually black and creamy white. The backswimmer has to breathe the free air and therefore must come to the surface occasionally for a fresh supply. As it swims down from the surface of the water the back part of the body has a silvery appearance, which is caused by the air clinging to the body and under the wings. It is held there by fine hairs. The insect takes this supply of air under water with it, enabling it to stay submerged for some time. Most backswimmers feed on other water insects. Look for them in the mud among the vegetation growing at the edge of the water, in submerged masses of tangled roots, around submerged logs, and in the water under overhanging banks.

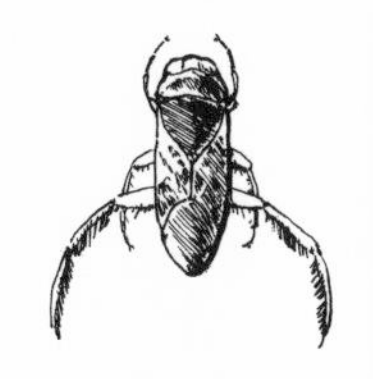

Backswimmer

Waterscorpion. These may be found in the quiet parts of streams and ponds — among the water weeds and trash — a long slender insect, dirty brown in color and having two long, slender, bristlelike breathing organs projecting from the tip of the abdomen. The last two pairs of legs are long and used in walking, while the front ones are used for capturing food. It feeds on water insects of many kinds, small fish, and even on other waterscorpions. Collect waterscorpions by moving your dip net strongly back and forth in the mud among the water plants.

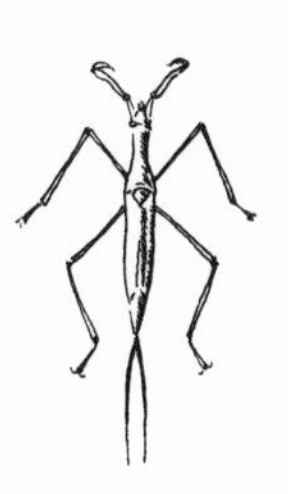

Water scorpion

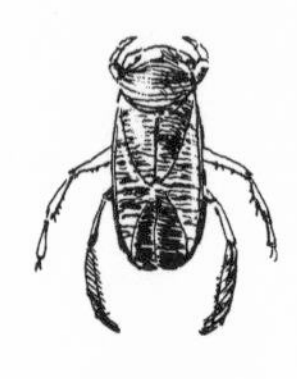

Water boatman

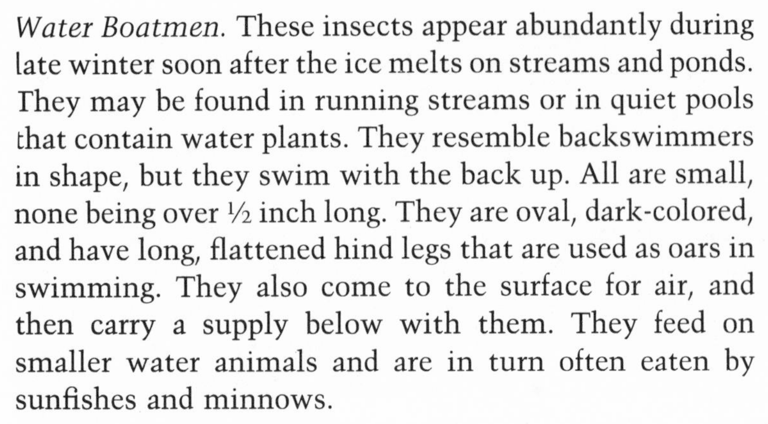

Water Boatmen. These insects appear abundantly during late winter soon after the ice melts on streams and ponds. They may be found in running streams or in quiet pools that contain water plants. They resemble backswimmers in shape, but they swim with the back up. All are small, none being over ½ inch long. They are oval, dark-colored, and have long, flattened hind legs that are used as oars in swimming. They also come to the surface for air, and then carry a supply below with them. They feed on smaller water animals and are in turn often eaten by sunfishes and minnows.

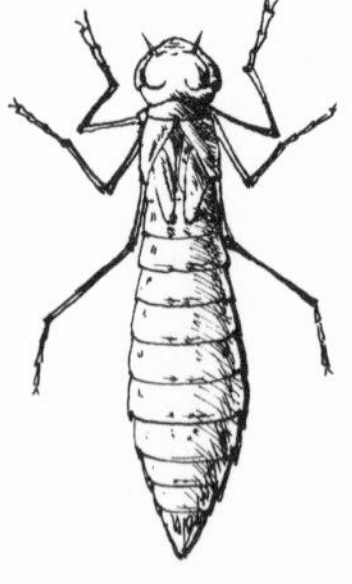

Dragonfly nymph

Dragonfly Nymphs. These nymphs are sluggish, mud-colored fellows that can be found at almost any time during the year and in almost any kind of aquatic situation. Some crawl about on the bottom while others burrow into the bottom. They are fierce creatures and make constant raids on the other water insects, even attacking animals about twice their size. After living for some time on the bottom, dragonfly nymphs leave the water by crawling up stems or other objects. There the old skin is shed and the full-grown insects appear.

Mosquito pupa

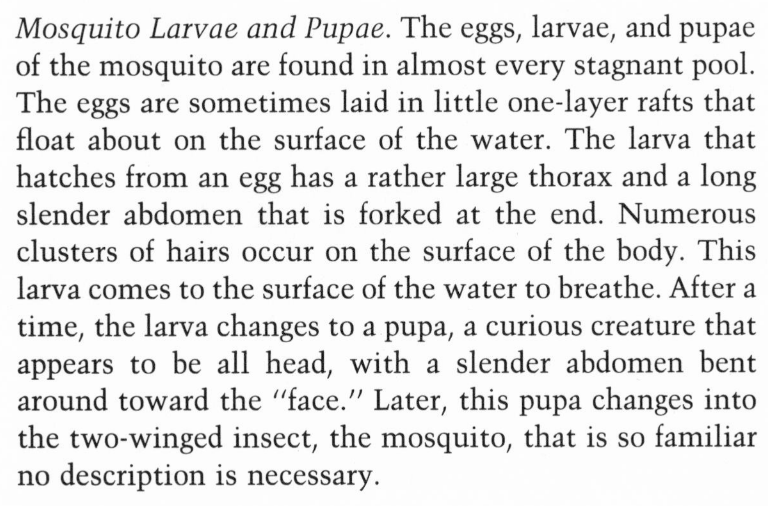

Mosquito Larvae and Pupae. The eggs, larvae, and pupae of the mosquito are found in almost every stagnant pool. The eggs are sometimes laid in little one-layer rafts that float about on the surface of the water. The larva that hatches from an egg has a rather large thorax and a long slender abdomen that is forked at the end. Numerous clusters of hairs occur on the surface of the body. This larva comes to the surface of the water to breathe. After a time, the larva changes to a pupa, a curious creature that appears to be all head, with a slender abdomen bent around toward the "face." Later, this pupa changes into the two-winged insect, the mosquito, that is so familiar no description is necessary.

Mosquito larva

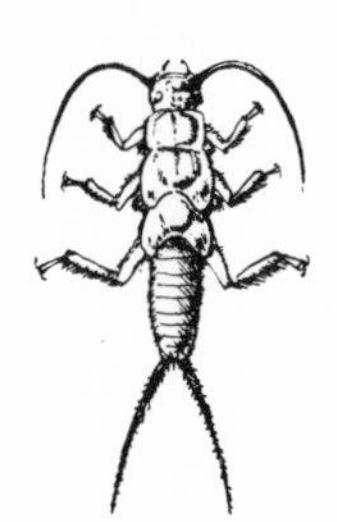

Stonefly larva

Stonefly Larvae. The larval form of the stonefly is found only in rapid streams, being most abundant in rapids and riffles where the water rushes over half-submerged rocks. Lift these stones suddenly and look carefully on the lower side. A flat larva — about ¾ inch long, with two long bristlelike antennae, two long bristlelike structures at the end of the abdomen, and tufts of branching gills at the bases of the legs—will often be found clinging to the rock. The legs are usually fringed with hairs. The larvae are very active and quickly hide themselves when disturbed. To collect them, pick them off the stone or wash them off into a jar. They cannot live except in running water. Adult stoneflies can be found near the rocky streams where their larvae live.

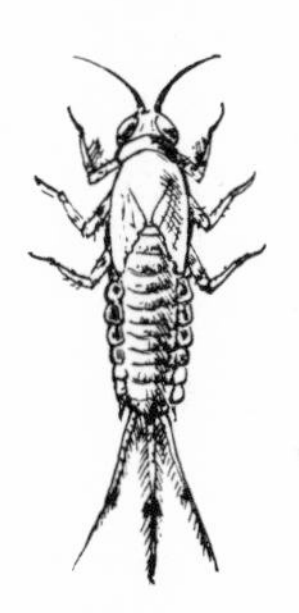

Mayfly nymph

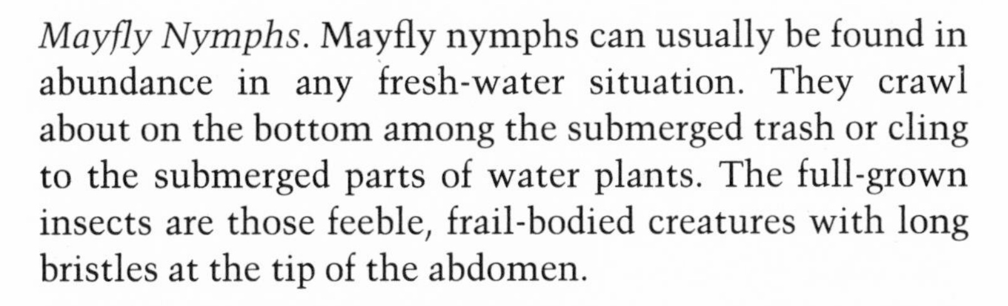

Mayfly Nymphs. Mayfly nymphs can usually be found in abundance in any fresh-water situation. They crawl about on the bottom among the submerged trash or cling to the submerged parts of water plants. The full-grown insects are those feeble, frail-bodied creatures with long bristles at the tip of the abdomen.

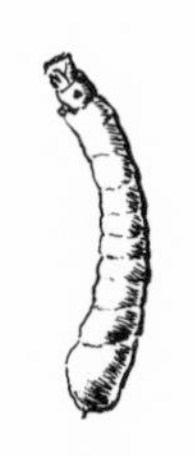

Black fly larva

Black Fly Larvae. When looking for stonefly larvae in rocky, swift-running streams, you will sometimes find clusters of squirming little black creatures attached to rocks or other smooth objects by the hind part of the body. These are black fly larvae. The free end hangs out into the current and has two brushes of hairs that take the food from the water. These larvae pass through a pupa stage and then hatch into those little black, blood-sucking, hump-backed flies we know so well.

Damselfly Nymphs. These nymphs are usually abundant in shallow pools, marshes, and the edges of streams and ponds where water plants are numerous. They crawl about among the submerged plant stems and feed on

Damselfly nymph

small water insects that come within their reach. After living in this way for a time, they crawl out of the water onto a stem and there change into adults. These insects look like small dragonflies but they have front and hind wings alike.

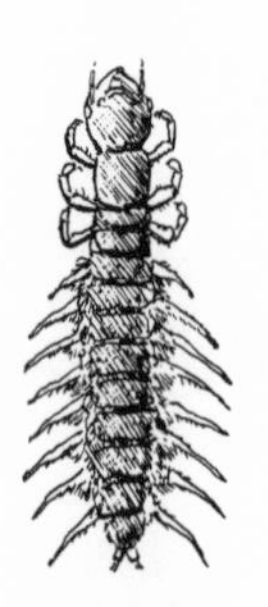
Dobsonfly larva

Dobsonfly Larvae (Hellgrammites). Dip-net sweepings among the rocks in streams sometimes bring up a creature with tapered projections along the sides of the abdomen. The head bears a pair of strong jaws and on the thorax are three pairs of legs. It feeds on other water insects. The full-grown dobsonfly is a large net-winged insect with long antennae and bulging eyes. It is often killed around electric lights at night in spring and summer.

Crane Fly Larvae. These footless, wormlike, dirty-brown larvae are often found in moss, slime, or decaying leaves on the wet banks of streams very near the edge of the water. They may also be found in the wet, rotten parts of partly submerged logs. The head is small and inconspicuous, while the tip of the abdomen usually bears several fleshy projections surrounding two large dark circular breathing pores. The larvae feed on decaying vegetation. The pupa differs from the larva in having a distinct head on the tip of which are two long breathing tubes. The adult crane fly is that long-legged, two-winged insect which flies about in damp shady places and looks like a huge mosquito.

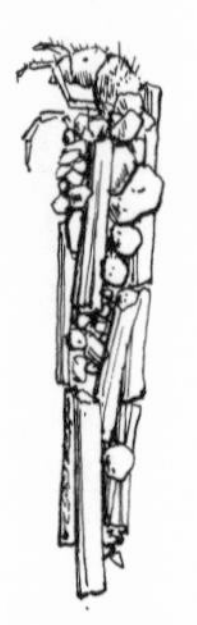
Caddisfly larva

Caddisfly Larvae. Sweeping a dip net in any kind of aquatic situation is likely to bring up some curious bits of wood or stone that may at first escape the eye and be cast aside with the debris. Possibly, the collector will be startled to see some of these little masses of stones and sticks move. These are the cases or houses of the caddisfly larvae, sometimes called caddis worms. Further search about the collecting grounds will reveal the surprising variety in the way in which these cases are built. Some are made of small pebbles and sand; some are made of little sticks crossed in such a way as to make a tiny log-cabin affair; some are made of sticks placed lengthwise; some are made of bits of leaves and grass, and so on. Although very rough on the outside, the cavity on the inside is lined with smooth silk. The dark-headed larva lives in this cavity and carries the case about with it. It moves from place to place by thrusting the head and legs out through the opening of the case. These creatures feed on aquatic plants. After a certain period of growth, the larva fastens the case and changes into a pupa. The pupa finally leaves the case, climbs up out of the water on a stem or other object, and there hatches into an adult. It is a brown or grayish mothlike insect with long thready antennae and long, rather narrow wings that have very fine hairs scattered over the surface. These adults can be collected around lights at night in summer.

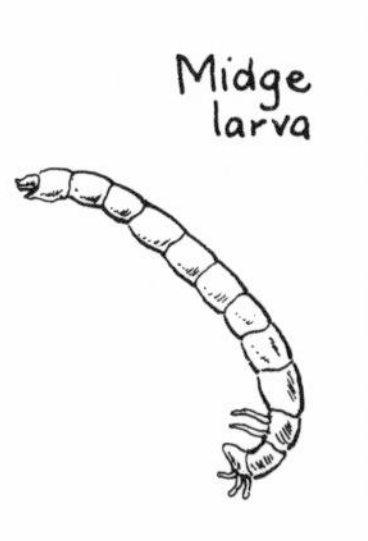

Midge Larvae. In dip-net sweepings of the bottom of weedy ponds or other bodies of quiet water, some blood-red, wormlike creatures will often be found wriggling in the slime and among the decaying leaves in the bottom of the net. Each has a long slender jointed body with a pair of legs on the first joint and a pair on the last joint. The section before the last joint usually bears two pairs of breathing organs on the lower side. These larvae move about by an irregular looping of the body from one side to the other. They live in a sort of tube made of rubbish. They will rebuild their tubes and after a time change into the pupa stage, which is very much like the pupa stage of the mosquito except that it has branching gills on top of the thorax. The pupa finally becomes an adult midge, which looks very much like a mosquito.

Galls

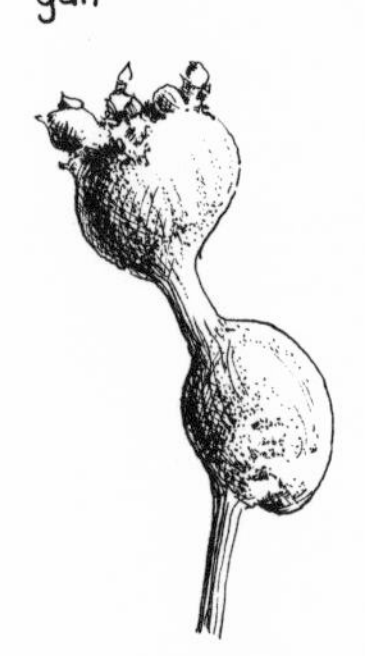

Wild cherry bud gall

A green little world
With me at its heart!
A house grown by magic,
Of a green stem, a part.

My walls give me food
And protect me from foes,
I eat at my leisure,
In safety repose.

My house hath no window,
'Tis dark as the night!
But I make me a door
And batten it tight.

And when my wings grow
I throw wide my door!
And to my green castle
I return never more.

Anna Bodsford Comstock
1913

You have probably seen many galls, but you may not have known what they were. A gall is a growth or swelling on the stem of a plant. It is a result of activity of a specific organism or creature. In the United States there are approximately 2000 species of gall makers — insects, mites, fungi, and bacteria. Galls can be found in fields, forests, or marshes. They occur on plant buds, leaves. flowers, twigs, roots, and under bark. The gall affects a specific area of one kind of plant. Each gall resembles every other gall made by the species. There are rare exceptions of gall makers producing galls on different parts of plants. Most of the galls you are likely to find in a winter search are caused by insects.

Some insect galls are formed when an insect lays its eggs on the plant. An example of this is the little fly, which lays its eggs on the tip of the growing stem of the goldenrod. When it leaves its eggs, a chemical is also left. This chemical affects the normal growth of the plant. The result is a tip that has swollen. The swelling contains all the leaves that would have grown along the stem during normal growth.

In spring a small wasp lays her eggs on an oak leaf. The larva hatches and begins to eat into the leaf vein. As it eats, it gives off a chemical which is part of its natural digestive process. The plant reacts to that chemical by growing vegetable fibers out from the point where the larva rests. A smooth thin round covering grows larger and larger around the larva. It remains snug and protected inside.

Other galls are formed by larvae that hatch from eggs laid on the ground. The larvae then find their way to their specific area on a particular plant.

The sawfly has an ovipositor located at the tip of the abdomen. With it, it cuts a slit into the twig of the plant and lays its eggs. A chemical given off during the process causes an irritation to the plant resulting in a gall.

The growth caused by the insect affects a portion of the plant, which then swells and encircles the organism. The gall maker is provided with a home that protects it from predators and parasites and is also a concentrated food supply. The gall is a snug home for the insect to spend the winter and develop in. In the spring the adult emerges to lay eggs, which continue the cycle and the species. In some cases the adult leaves the gall and winters in another place.

The gall insect sometimes shares his winter home. The willow pine gall, for example, has scales that form around the gall maker. Under the scales can be found aphids, springtails, midges, mites, spiders, and centipedes. They do not bother the gall insect in any way; they merely share its home, for it offers protection against the winter elements. Woodpeckers, squirrels, mice, and chickadees include larvae extracted from galls in their diets. If you find a goldenrod ball gall with a freshly drilled hole, it is probably the result of a hairy or downy woodpecker. To these small woodpeckers, the larva is a plump morsel of food. Mice or squirrels pull, tear, or chew away a chunk of the gall to get at the food inside.

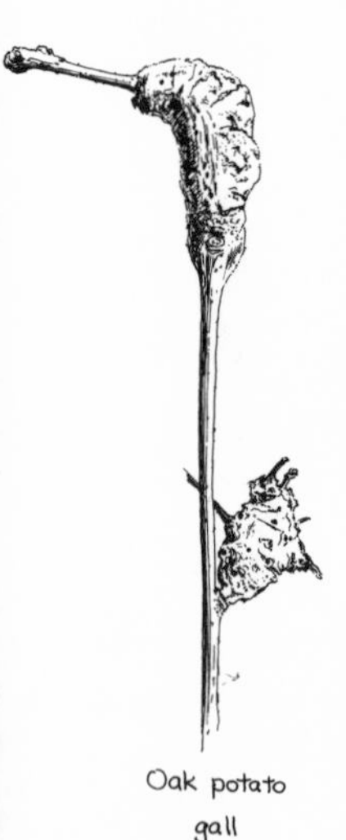
Oak potato gall

Galls can be found anywhere that plants grow. A good place to look is on oak trees, for oak trees retain galls even after their leaves have fallen. There are more than 800 species of galls associated with oak trees.

If you wish to study galls, it is possible to mount a collection or keep galls for observation. If you'd like to collect a variety of galls and mount them, be certain to gather two of each species. This will enable you to study and dissect one and have the other for display. Tape the specimens on a 5- by 8-inch index card and label with information about the gall. Cutting a portion of the stem along with the gall will make it easier to mount.

Gall Observation

If you'd like to keep galls throughout the winter for observation and to see the adults or larvae emerge in the spring, it is very important to keep them under proper conditions. A breeding chamber can easily be constructed. Keep in mind a few important guidelines. An observation chamber must reproduce living conditions that are as close to normal as possible.

Put soil in a wide-mouthed jar. A gallon jar is the best size. Do not house more than one gall in each container.

Making a Mounted Gall Collection

Here is the information that would be valuable to keep for a mounted gall collection. The date collected and other data can be written on the back of the card.

Where did you find the gall?

in forest, field, marsh, etc.
name of the plant
where found on the host plant

What does it look like?

size, shape, color
texture
general appearance

What's inside?

draw
identify (if you can)
- egg
- larva
- adult

This will provide more control in your study and observation and avoid confusion. Collect the gall by cutting a portion of the twig or stem 4 to 6 inches long. In the bottom of the jar a layer of soil should be put over a layer of sand. Stick the twig containing the gall into the soil. Cover the jar opening with cheesecloth. Keep the soil moist by adding water periodically. You may want to sterilize the soil before putting it into the jar. This will avoid the possibility of other insects emerging from the soil. Soil can be sterilized quite simply by heating it to 250 degrees in the oven.

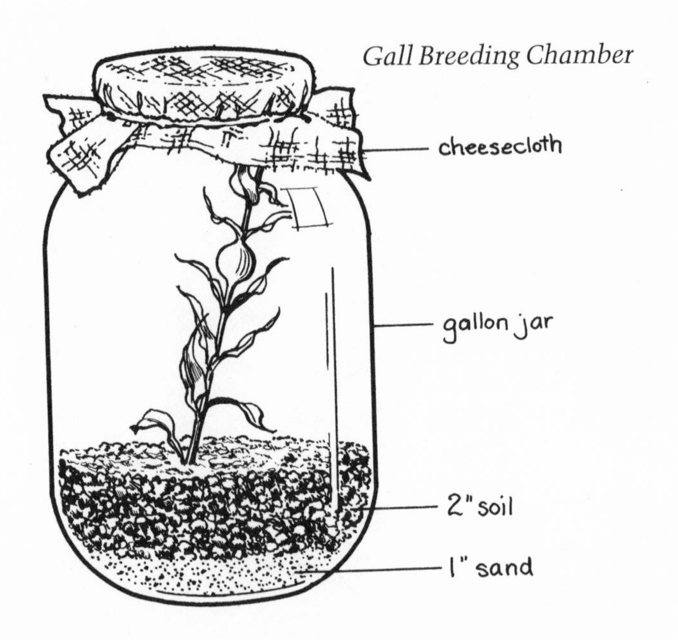

Gall Breeding Chamber

The soil is very important because the larvae of some gall insects leave the galls and enter the soil before changing into an adult form. It is essential that you provide a proper habitat for those gall insects that require this condition. Minimize temperature extremes by keeping the breeding chamber out of direct sunlight and away from heat sources. Also keep the gall from drying out. The jar should be kept outdoors until warmer weather arrives to approximate normal conditions.

There are some galls that share their winter homes with other small creatures. If you watch closely on a daily basis, you will be able to see some of these tenants. Be careful not to confuse these small creatures with the true gall maker.

Collect a variety of galls. Cut each one in half and probe the inner contents. How is the gall structured? What is the inside made of? What are the similarities and differences among the galls?

Create a Gall

After you have investigated a number of galls to learn about how they are structured, try this experiment to determine if a larva can continue to develop if it is removed from its gall. Find a gall containing a larva. It will be necessary to make a new home for the larva. Remember that the gall provides protection from enemies as well as a food supply for the gall insect.

Extract the larva from its home and place the larva in a human-made gall. The substitute home can be made by

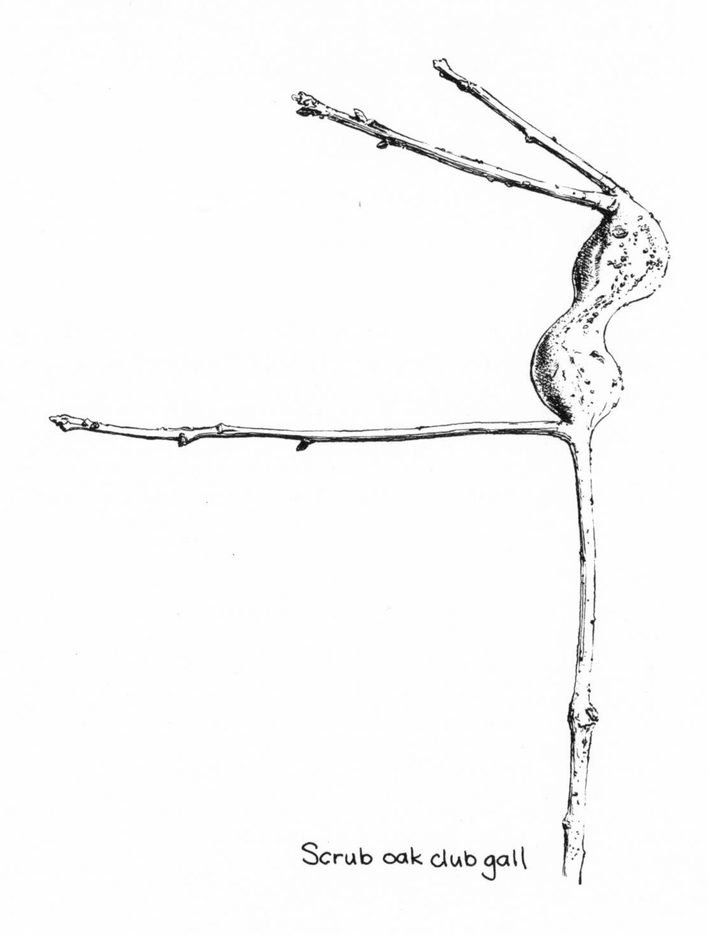

wrapping the larva in soft and absorbent material such as cotton, cloth, foam rubber, Styrofoam, or any other material that you think will provide the qualities of its natural home. The larva should be enclosed in the home with a small amount of food, such as a cooked vegetable or other soft food that will not spoil rapidly. It will have to be replenished occasionally. Place your home-made gall in a jar and provide the conditions that were outlined for the breeding chamber, covering it with cheesecloth and keeping the gall moist.

Be patient. The larva still must develop before it emerges. It may be days or months before you see whether your experiment was successful.

Some Common Galls of the Northeast and North Central United States and Southern Canada

Included below is information about some of the common galls you are likely to find in your winter wanderings. Resources listed at the end of this book provide more information about galls and gall makers.

Oak Apple Gall. A female wasp lays an egg on a leaf in the spring by injecting her ovipositor into the leaf stem. Along with the egg a chemical irritant is also injected. This chemical begins the gall formation. The larva hatches from the egg and eats its way into the leaf vein. A chemical is expelled from the mouth of the larva during this feeding activity. It causes vegetable fibers to grow out in a radiating fashion with the larva at their center. A smooth thin covering encloses the fibers and larva, growing larger and larger. Meanwhile, the larva completes growth, changes to a pupa, and emerges as a tiny ⅛-inch

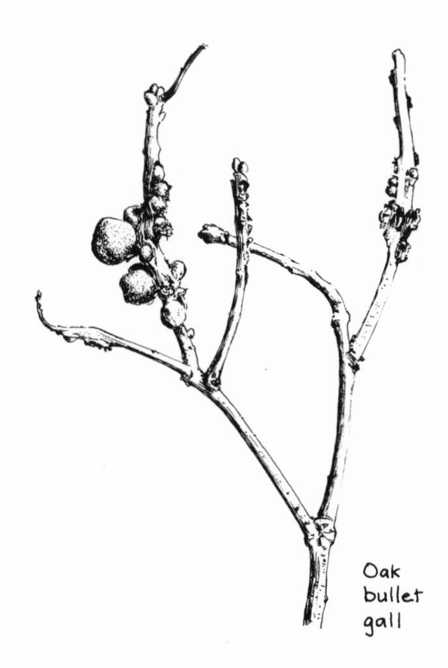

long wasp. The leaf may fall to the ground but the cycle continues if the gall is completely formed.

Oak galls are easy to find because many oak leaves remain on the branches throughout winter. Other oak galls caused by the activities of a wasp species are the oak bullet gall and the oak hedgehog gall.

Pine Willow Gall. A small fly (the midge) lays her eggs in the spring on an opening branch bud of the willow. The eggs hatch into maggots (larvae), which secrete a chemical. The secretion stops the external growth of the twig. The leaves of the branch are stunted and become overlapping scales that make up the outside covering of the gall. The maggot emerges in the spring as a tiny two-winged fly. The scales that make up the outside covering are used as homes in winter by springtails, mites, spiders, aphids, and other small creatures.

Goldenrod ball gall

Another common group of galls, found often in fields and other open areas, is the goldenrod galls.

Goldenrod Ball Gall. The goldenrod ball gall forms on the Canada goldenrod as a result of an egg deposited by a fly. The cream-colored larva that hatches from the egg eats its way to the center of the stem and discharges from its mouth a chemical that causes the gall to form around the larva. The larva emerges in late April as a fly, the size of a house fly, with reddish-brown wings and white markings. The fly has no teeth and cannot bite its way out of the gall. However, the larva has prepared an exit, chewing a tunnel almost to the surface. The fly needs only to push out the thin layer of the plant skin in order to emerge. The goldenrod ball gall is an excellent sample to keep in an observation jar.

Goldenrod Spindle Gall. The goldenrod spindle gall is formed on the Canada goldenrod by the activity of a brown and gray moth that emerges in the fall, lays her eggs on the stem of the goldenrod, and then dies. The eggs hatch the following spring. The caterpillars that develop from the eggs find their way to a living goldenrod, where they eat their way into a bud and down the stem. The moth caterpillar eats its way almost to the outer surface of the gall before it pupates. It has tapered a hole that will be used when it is time to leave the gall. The tapered hole makes it difficult for predators to enter but easy for the toothless adult moth to push its way out. Usually, the gall will be empty in winter. You can find empty pupa skins inside these galls and an open exit hole. In some areas of the United States an adult moth will winter in the gall.

Goldenrod Tapered Gall. This gall resembles the spindle gall but is more elongated. It is located higher on the stem and is caused by a moth. In winter it may contain a caterpillar or pupa.

Goldenrod Bunch Gall. The development of this particular gall is the result of the activities of a gnat-sized fly that lays her eggs on the goldenrod in June. When an egg hatches, a secreted chemical causes the plant to stop growing. The leaves that would have grown along the stem form the outside of the gall, growing around the larva. The larva grows, pupates, and emerges as an adult before winter. It hibernates in another place during winter. Other small creatures may winter in the gall.

Blackberry Knot Gall. The blackberry knot gall is caused by a wasp. The gall has many cells, each containing a white wasp larva in winter. The gall has a bumpy, woody texture. It is found on the stem of a blackberry bush.

Raspberry Knot Gall. The raspberry knot gall is similar to the blackberry knot gall. It is caused by the activity of a wasp related to the one that causes the blackberry knot gall.

Mossy Rose Gall. This type of gall is located on a rose bush branch. It contains many hard cells. Each cell contains a white wasp larva in winter.

Black Knot Gall. This gall is found on wild cherry trees. It is caused by a fungus and can kill the branch it forms on.

If you find a gall on an unknown plant, these guidelines may help you in determining some information about the inhabitant.

Gall Caterpillars: Six legs on thorax, head, no prolegs on abdomen.

Gall Wasp and Fly Larva: White, no legs.

Caterpillar: White, wormlike insect with six short legs.

Fly Larva: May be yellow, red, orange, or salmon.

6. Exploring Water Communities in Winter

In winter, when shallow pools of water freeze and frost penetrates into the wet ground of marshlands, animal activity is altered. Many of the marsh inhabitants hibernate. The cold-blooded turtles, water snakes, frogs, and salamanders are securely burrowed into the mud at the bottom of ponds and streams. Cold-blooded animals cannot maintain as steady a body temperature as mammals and birds can. Thus, they are very vulnerable to sudden temperature changes. Since bodies of water are slow to respond to atmospheric temperature changes, they offer a perfect, moderate environment for many reptiles and amphibians.

Along the pond and lake edges, muskrats carve burrows in banks. They feed on stockpiles of roots and stalks beneath the ice.

In nearby fields, moles travel through winding tunnels in search of grubs and insects. Their tunnels extend beyond the frost line, for they seek earthworms, which have gone deep into the soil to escape the cold. The mole spends much of its life traveling the maze of subterranean canals it has dug.

The seed- and bark-eating meadow mice have also etched intertwining pathways. These are beneath a blanket of snow, rather than through the soil.

Plants stiffly protrude through the crust of snow and offer seeds to juncos, tree sparrows, and snow buntings.

The snowy owl hunts by day in the marsh. Mice and small birds satisfy its palate. Dressed in white, it waits on a hummock of sedge or a tree stump. Weasels, also in white coats, dive under the snow and follow mice tunnels in search of a meal. At night, the fox prowls the marsh and captures mice. The snowy owl, weasel, and fox are all predators. They keep the meadow mice or voles from overpopulating the landscape.

Most ponds will not freeze solidly to the bottom unless they are very shallow. Bodies of water maintain a relatively even temperature despite atmospheric extremes. The heating and cooling process for a lake or pond occurs much more slowly than in the surrounding countryside. In the fall, when cooler temperatures remain steady, water in a pond or lake gradually cools. As water cools, it contracts and becomes denser because the motion of water molecules slows. This allows the molecules to pack tightly together and become heavier than warm water. Water is heaviest at 39°F, or 4°C. When it reaches this temperature it sinks to the bottom and flushes up the warmer water beneath. A lake or pond "turns over" like this once in the fall and once in the spring. The water that has been displaced from the bottom soon cools to 32°F and freezes in crystals of ice. This layer of ice forms a protective covering and provides a habitat under the ice where many plants and animals can survive. Salt water freezes at a lower temperature than fresh water because of the dissolved salts and minerals it contains.

Green plants use sunlight and give off oxygen in the food-making process called photosynthesis. Plants produce little or no food during the winter as a result of the amount of sunlight available on the shortened winter days. The plants, therefore, do not release as large amounts of oxygen as they do in other seasons. If the ice on the pond is covered with snow, sunlight may be kept completely from the green water plants and therefore less oxygen is available in winter. Many plants die in winter because they do not receive an adequate amount of light. The decaying plants use even more oxygen.

Fortunately, cold water holds more oxygen than warm water, enabling the many fish, insects, nymphs, and other water animals to survive in winter when the production of oxygen from green plants is minimal. As the water gets colder, the cold-blooded animals also become less active and require less oxygen.

Moving stream water is constantly exposed to the air, causing it to be rich in oxygen. Stream water also retains a relatively even temperature at both the top and bottom because of the mixing of water and air as it pours and tumbles over rocks.

Some floating water plants, such as duckweed, have an interesting solution to the food problem. They accumulate food in the form of starch during the fall. They sink to the bottom as the water cools. When the starch has been used up, duckweed floats to the surface. By this time, it is usually spring and much of the ice has melted.

In addition to the insect inhabitants of water communities you may also find crayfish and cyclops. Here are some questions to ask about each creature you find.

What are its physical features? Does it have a head,

thorax, abdomen, pads? Does it move? How? Can you tell what it eats by how it looks? What does it eat? What eats it?

Are there any creatures frozen in the ice on the surface of a pond? If there are, are they dead or alive?

Collect some pieces of ice from the pond's surface. Put the ice in a glass bowl or dish. Let the ice melt slowly at room temperature. When it has completely melted, let the water sit until it is room temperature. Can you observe any creatures in the water? Are they dead or alive? Use a magnifying lens, microscope, or dissecting scope and examine a small quantity of water in a glass dish or on a microscope slide. Place the container against a dark background and then a light background so that the light- and dark-colored creatures can be seen more easily.

Collect ice from along a shallow stream, or near the edge of a pond where the ice extends to the bottom. Melt this sample using the same procedure. Observe, asking the same questions as above. Compare your results. Try this same activity with ice taken from a marsh.

Look for tracks in snow or mud around the frozen pond, or in the snow covering the ice. What made them? Draw what you find. Do you find any scat? Check on other days to see if other animals have been moving in the area. Have you seen the animal that left its signature near the pond? Can you tell from the track story what the animal was doing near the pond? Follow the tracks. Where do they lead? To a feeding place, a den? Was the animal walking, running, or feeding?

Fish vary from species to species in their response to the colder water and other conditions of winter. Some fish prefer cold water and remain active during winter, while others go to deeper water where the temperature is warmer. Still others migrate south to a warmer ocean climate. Others remain dormant, buried in the mud at the bottom of the pond.

Cod, halibut, and herring winter in their range in the colder salt water off the North Atlantic coast. Mackerel seek deeper, warmer salt water and become less active in winter. Weakfish migrate south with the warmer ocean currents, while bluefish go deeper in warmer water offshore. Atlantic salmon are unique in their behavior. They live in the ocean from two to four years. In spring the adults will travel up rivers to where they were born, reaching their destination by fall. The eggs laid by the females in nests made at the bottom of shallow water remain in the nests through the winter and hatch the following spring. After two years in the fresh water, the young salmon travel to the sea.

Freshwater fish also demonstrate this variation in winter behavior. Bass spend the winter season in deeper water in a dormant state on the bottom and take shelter under rocks and locks. Horned pouts (bullheads) bury themselves in the bottom mud or under debris. Northern pike are active in the winter in deeper warmer water of ponds and lakes. Brook trout, also active in winter, prefer cold fast-flowing streams.

Amphibians are cold-blooded and hibernate during winter. Their body processes slow down, and less oxygen is needed. The oxygen used is absorbed through the skin and is sufficient to sustain life. Many amphibians hibernate in the pond. The leopard frog crawls under a rock or log in the bottom mud of ponds. It can survive even if frozen in the ice, as long as it is not frozen through.

The bullfrog remains a tadpole for two or three years of its life. The tadpole and the adult frog hibernate during winter under the mud and bottom debris of the pond.

Turtles are reptiles, which also hibernate during the win-

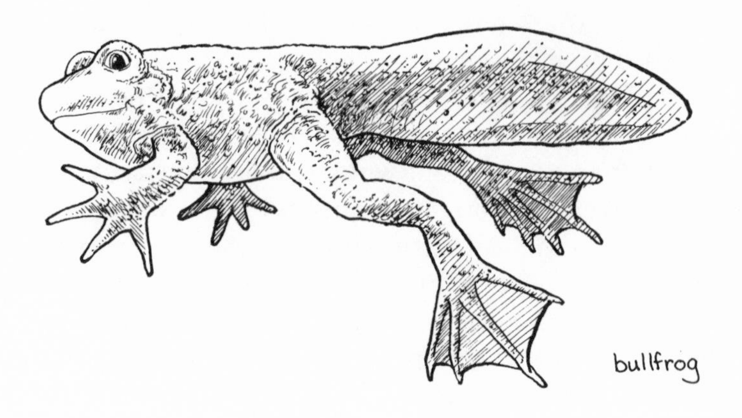

ter season. They are cold-blooded. Their body processes slow down and they too absorb oxygen through their skin. The snapping turtle in the colder part of its range will hibernate in mud underwater in rivers, ponds, and lakes. The painted turtle also hibernates in the bottom mud of ponds and slow-moving streams.

One of the most interesting animals of the pond is the beaver. The beaver is the largest rodent in North America, weighing up to 60 pounds. Although it travels on land to gather wood for food and to build dams and lodges, the beaver is very vulnerable to predators on dry land.

Beavers have the ability to change their surroundings to ensure their safety. By building a dam made of interwoven logs, debris, and mud across a stream, they create a pond. The depth of the water in the pond provides protection for the lodge they build of sticks and mud. The lodge entrances are underwater. Living quarters inside the lodge are above the water. The inside temperature of the lodge remains at 55° to 60°F throughout the winter.

During the fall, beavers collect branches that they store in an underwater cache, stuck in the mud near the entrance to the lodge. When ice covers the pond in winter they are assured of an adequate food supply. Once ice has formed on the pond the beaver spends the entire winter under the ice or in its lodge. A beaver is well adapted for life in the cold water. A coat of oil is spread over its thick coat of fur to waterproof the animal. Its wide tail and large hind feet aid in swimming underwater. The pond created by beavers not only provides a safe place for them and their young but also creates a habitat for numerous other aquatic organisms.

7. More Things to Do in Winter

Making Snowshoes

Try dropping into the snow a stone and an aluminum pie plate of the same weight. Or drop a stone into the snow, then tape the stone to a pie plate and drop it into the snow. Which one sinks in deeper? Searching for small creatures or following tracks of animals may take you into a field or wooded area where the snow is deep. You will be able to travel much more easily, stay drier, and enjoy yourself more if you can walk on the snow. Sinking up to your knees or deeper with each step can be exhausting and can quickly discourage even the most enthusiastic winter wanderer. As with the example of the stone and the plate, snowshoes spread the weight of your body over more surface area, preventing you from sinking in as deeply as you would if you were not wearing snowshoes.

Trace a snowshoe on a piece of paper. Trace your foot

on another piece of paper. You can see how much area supports your body weight with each type of shoe. If you don't have snowshoes and are not able to borrow a pair, you may want to make some. Here are simple directions for making inexpensive snowshoes.

Conifer-Branch Snowshoes

Snowshoes like these were made and used by many Indians who inhabited snow country in the Northeast and North Central United States. This method provides an excellent use for discarded Christmas trees. Branches of pine, cedar, fir, hemlock or spruce can be used. Because of its gummy, thick sap, red spruce seems to be the best choice.

Materials

Branches from any of the conifers listed above
Ball of twine
¼-inch-thick rope
Rawhide laces

Procedure

1. For each snowshoe, select two branches about 18 inches long (or find one branch with a natural fork). The branches should be about ¾-inch thick. Try to select branches that are relatively the same thickness the entire length; this will provide additional strength.

2. With twine, tie the two pieces together at the larger end. The branches usually have a natural curve. The bends can be faced out or in, but they should both face the same way.

3. Once the bases have been secured, bend the tops around to complete the outside frame. Overlap if the pieces form too large an oval. Tie the pieces to strengthen the entire outside frame.

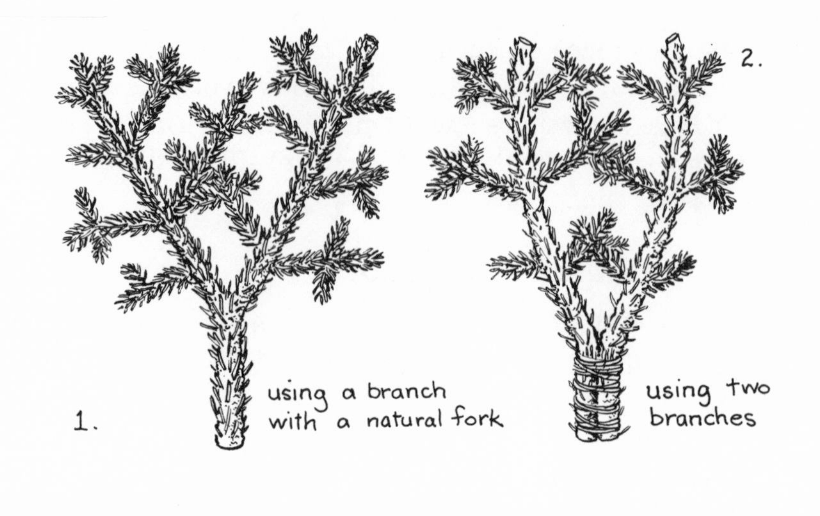

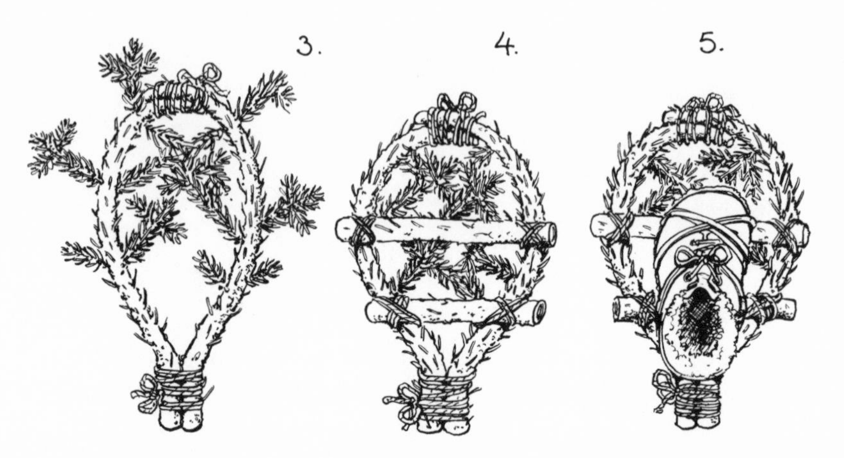

Conifer-branch Snowshoes

4. Form the desired shape by inserting two cross pieces; they need to be strong and relatively the same thickness along the entire length. They should overlap the outside by no more than 1 inch. Tie them to the outside frame with a strong ¼-inch rope.

5. More cross pieces can be added for strength and support. Support pieces can be added lengthwise as well.

Use rawhide laces to tie your boot in place. The snowshoes can be trimmed of needles, but the needles and extra branches are useful as webbing and should be woven in.

Wood-Frame Snowshoes

This method requires more materials than the previous one. The snowshoes may last longer, but this depends on the materials used and the way they are constructed.

Materials

Any lumber 1 to 2 inches wide and ⅜- to ½-inch thick
Leather straps
Nails; screws; or nuts and bolts
Hand drill

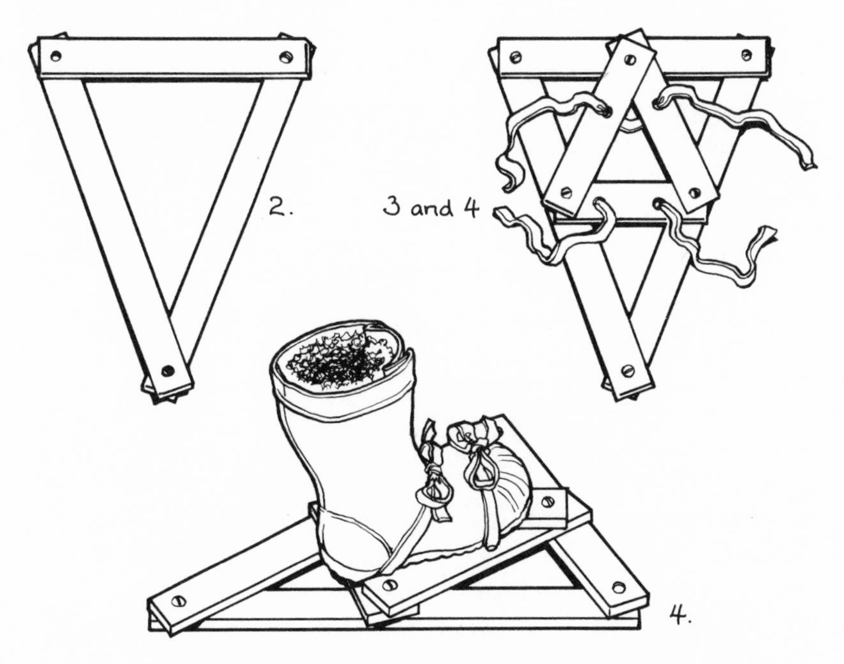

Wood-frame Snowshoes

Procedure

1. For one pair of snowshoes cut the lumber in the following quantities and lengths: four pieces 20 inches long, two 15 inches long, four 10 inches long, two 8 inches long.

2. Using two 20-inch pieces and one 15-inch piece, nail, screw, or bolt together each base frame as shown. If you use nuts and bolts, drill the holes first. (Nuts and bolts provide the strongest frame.)

3. Attach the smaller pieces to the base frame as shown.

4. String leather straps through drilled holes. These will be used to tie in and secure the boot.

5. Varnish the wood to preserve it and protect the snowshoes against damage done by water.

Plywood Snowshoes

The third method of making snowshoes requires two solid pieces of wood; ⅜-inch-thick plywood is a good choice.

Materials

Plywood
Drill
Coping saw or small hand saw
Leather straps
Stain or varnish

Procedure

1. Cut the wood into two oblong oval pieces about 18 inches long and 10 inches wide.

2. Draw patterns for the heel and toe holes.

3. Drill holes in the center of the pattern so that the

heel and toe holes can be cut using a saw. A hand jigsaw could also be used.

4. Cut the toe and heel holes.
5. Drill holes for the leather straps.
6. If you like, cut other holes to make the shoe lighter. If you choose to do this, be careful not to weaken the entire structure. Thinner wood may also be used, but wood less than 3/8-inch thick may be too weak. Stain or varnish the snowshoes to protect the wood from the constant contact with wet snow.

Snowshoe Games

Once you have made snowshoes, find others who have them or teach others to make them. Have races or relay games on snowshoes in an open field, up a hill, or along a logging road.

Many games that you play in other seasons can also be played in winter and are particularly fun if everyone wears snowshoes. Try tug of war, wheelbarrow races, jumping rope, potato-sack races, shadow tag, freeze tag, basketball with no dribbling, baseball, football, or any other games you think might be fun played on snowshoes.

Snow Games

Here are several games to play in the snow. Make up your own snow games, too.

Snow Throw

It is always fun to throw snowballs. Why not make a game out of it? Make a snow throw by hanging a loop made from a coat hanger on a branch of a tree. Throw snowballs through the loop from varying distances. A good idea is to hang the loop from a tree in front of a hill or a rise. Throwing into the hill will be much safer. Set a basket or pail on the surface of the snow. From varying distances, try tossing your snowball into the container.

Fox and Hare

Play an old New England game called fox and hare. Tramp down a wheel with spokes in fresh snow. One person is the fox. The remaining people are the hares. No one may run off the trampled paths. The fox tries to catch the hares. When a hare is caught he must go to the center and stay there. Increasing the number of foxes is a variation. Another way the game can be played is to enable a caught hare to be freed if touched by an uncaught hare. This game is best played with about twenty people. So teach it to your class or to a group of friends at a winter party. It is an excellent game for communicating the concepts of predator and prey. Increasing the number of foxes will decrease the number of hares faster. The more hares there are, the easier it is for the fox to catch them.

Snow Snake

A favorite game of the Iroquois Indians was throwing the "snow snake," a smooth stick, 4 to 6 feet long, with an upturned end — like the shape of a cross-country ski, but narrower. A hickory or ash branch with the bark stripped from it is good to use.

Make a trail across a field or down a hill. By dragging a log, a trail like a rain gutter can easily be formed. Don't step in the gulley. Wetting the trail and letting it freeze overnight, as the Indians used to do, will provide a fast run.

The snake is shoved along into the trail from a starting

point. This can be played with others. Iroquois played with teams of six to see who could slide the snake the farthest. Some used to slide the snake more than half a mile on smooth lake surfaces.

Foot on a Log

How many people can get one foot on a log, tree stump, or piece of firewood? The other foot cannot touch the snow for at least 5 seconds! How many can you get on a log? Try it with a group of friends. Invent your own variations.

Other Snow Activities

Snow Candles

Dig a mold having the desired shape of the finished candle. Remember, snow is porous and the mold dug in the snow should be packed. If the snow is wet, this won't be a problem. If the snow is old or dry light powder, it may be more difficult to work with. Old snow produces some extremely interesting shapes, so try this in different types of snows and discover the various effects of hot wax on snow and ice.

Prepare the wax as you would to make candles indoors. Melt the paraffin (preferably in an old double boiler), and add crayons to give the wax color. When the wax has completely melted, allow it to cool somewhat. Then pour the wax into the snow mold. When the wax begins to get hard and cloudy, push a straight piece of coat hanger into it where you wish the wick to go. Allow the candle to harden. When it has completely hardened (about 25 minutes) take the candle inside and put the wick into the hole made by the wire. (Candlewick can be purchased at a hardware store or hobby shop.) Additional wax can be poured around the wick to seal the hole. You may want to try color layering or any other design variations you can think of. You will be amazed at the number of patterns that can be made by the snow and wax.

Snow Taffy

Boil maple syrup until it is very thick. Pour the hot syrup over clean snow that you've put in a cup. If your hands are clean and you can wait to eat the sweetened snow, form taffy by mixing and pulling the mixture.

Snow Shadows

On a bright sunny day, the shadows produced on the snow can provide enjoyment. Try to make various shapes, first using your entire body, then just your hands. How long can you make your shadow? How short? Use twigs or other materials to make shadows of animals. Put on a shadow play with some friends. Try shadow play at various times of day.

Snow Sculptures

When the temperature is below freezing, shape sculptures by digging snow and forming an animal figure. Wet snow is best for packing. Roll a ball of snow for the main body. Use sticks as bases for limbs and head; pack snow around these bases. Sculptures can be formed in the shape of squirrels, birds, or any animal you'd like. To form an icy coating on your sculpture, spray water from a spray bottle; this will help it last longer.

Igloo

Build an igloo or snow fort. This is a great way to use snow that has been plowed or shoveled into a pile. Invent a particular shape for the structure. You can build a scale model on a day when a fierce storm is raging and the

plows are busy piling the snow for you. Try to duplicate your scale model when you get outside and begin building. That old chunky snow from the piles is strong and will provide sturdy walls. When you have completed the structure, take temperatures inside and outside. How do the temperatures of the outside air and the inside of the igloo compare? Take the temperature readings on days with varying degrees of coldness.

Shelters

Lean branches against the lower limbs of a tree. Weave evergreen branches among and between them. Falling snow will form a blanketlike covering.

January Sky

The cold, clear nights of winter are very good for star viewing. It is one of the best seasons for learning the constellations. Information about them is available in the sources listed at the end of this book. A stargazing party can be a fun way for you and your friends to familiarize yourselves with the wonders of the night-time winter sky.

Appendix
Bibliographies
Index

Appendix

Track Story

The track story written below corresponds with the tale told in track language on page 33. After trying to read the tale in tracks, read the written story below to find out exactly what happened.

Nightfall approaches and the "night crew" of nocturnal animals begins to move about in the forest. The white-footed mouse emerges on the snow surface in search of buds, seeds, and bark to eat. He is quickly caught in the talons of the silent flying screech owl.

Night has fallen. In the forest many animals are becoming active for the first time today. In the dark of night, the red fox travels across the snow, stopping momentarily to dine on some dried blackberries. A snowshoe hare is startled by the fox's movement and flees with the fox in close pursuit. The deep snow is an advantage to the hare and it gains on the fox. The hare approaches its nest in a thicket and safety seems assured for tonight. At the last moment the sweeping talons of the great horned owl clutch the hare. The red fox stops abruptly in the cold night air.

This story will be told again in the morning by the various animals' tracks. The delicate print of the white-footed mouse has been interrupted by the talons and wing tips of the screech owl that have punctured the snow cover. The stride of the red fox nearly erases the tracks of the fleeing hare, before both are interrupted by the plunge of the great horned owl.

Wind Scale Chart

DESCRIPTION	MILES PER HOUR	TYPE OF WIND
Smoke rises straight up; leaves are still.	Less than 1	Calm
Leaves on trees barely rustle.	2–7	Slight Breeze
Leaves on twigs in motion; flags snapping.	8–12	Gentle Breeze
Dust and loose papers flying, small branches swaying.	13–18	Moderate Breeze
Small trees and leaves swaying; crests appearing on waves.	19–24	Fresh Breeze
Large branches in motion; whistling heard in telephone wires.	25–31	Strong Wind
Whole trees swaying; hard to walk against wind.	32–38	High Wind
Twigs broken off tree branches.	39–46	Gale
Branches of trees broken; signs blown down.	47–54	Strong Gale
Trees uprooted; barn roofs torn off; buildings damaged	55–75	Whole Gale
Buildings destroyed; trains overturned; telephone poles snapped off; automobiles lifted off highways.	More than 75	Hurricane

Mammals of the Northeast and North Central United States and Southern Canada

Bats
- Big Brown M and H
- Eastern Pipistrel (pygmy) M and H
- Hoary
- Indiana Myotis H
- Keen Myotis H
- Little Brown Myotis M then H
- Red M
- Silver-haired M
- Small-footed Myotis H

Black Bears WS

Cats
- Bobcat
- Eastern Cougar
- Lynx

Dogs, Wolves, and Foxes
- Eastern Coyote
- Gray Fox
- Red Fox
- Timber Wolf

Hares and Rabbits
- Eastern Cottontail
- New England Cottontail
- Snowshoe Hare

Hoofed Animals
- Moose
- Whitetail Deer

Moles
- Common Western
- Hairytail
- Starnose

Rodents
- Beaver
- Chipmunk WS/H
- Lemming
  - Northern Bog
  - Southern Bog
- Mouse
  - Deer
  - House or Meadow
  - Meadow Jumping H
  - White-footed
  - Woodland Jumping H
- Muskrat
- Porcupine
- Rat
  - Eastern Woodrat

WS — Winter Sleepers H — True Hibernators M — Migrators

Squirrels
- Flying
- Gray
- Northern Red
- Southern Red

Voles
- Boreal
- Meadow
- Pine
- Redback

Woodchuck H

Shrews
- Longtail
- Masked
- Pygmy
- Shorttail
- Water

Weasel Family WS
- Badgers
- Fisher
- Marten
- Mink
- River Otter
- Skunk
  - Spotted WS
  - Striped WS
- Weasels
  - Bonaparte's
  - Least
  - New York
  - Northern Longtail
  - Shorttail

AQUATIC MAMMALS

Dolphins and Porpoises
- Atlantic Bottlenose Dolphin
- Atlantic Harbor Porpoise
- Atlantic Killer Whale
- Atlantic White-sided Dolphin

Seals
- Harbor

Whales
- Atlantic Right Whale M
- Finback M
- Humpback M
- Minke M

Some Plant- and Seed-Eating Birds and Their Preferred Foods

Dark-eyed Junco, White-throated Sparrow: *Trees:* Yellow birch, wild cherry, hemlock
Weeds: Crabgrass, ragweed, pigweed, bustlegrass, knotweed, goldenrod.

Tree Sparrow (Primarily ground feeders): Weeds and grasses (90% of winter diet), smartweed, buckwheat, knotweed, lamb's-quarter, ragweed.

Mourning Dove: Bristlegrass, pokeweed, chuckweed, knotweed, ragweed, crabgrass, and agricultural grains.

Snow Bunting: Pigweed, knotweed, bulrush, ragweed, pomegrass.

Ring-necked Pheasant, Bobwhite Quail: Ragweed, bristlegrass, smartweed, sumac berries.

Horned Lark: Ragweed, pigweed, knotweed, bristlegrass, crabgrass, timothy, sunflower, agricultural grains.

Crow and Starling: Sumac, bayberry, poison ivy, weeds and grass seeds, sunflower, agricultural grains.

American Goldfinch: *Trees:* Pitch pine, apple, gray birch, alder
Weeds: Chicory, burdock, thistle, ragweed, bristlegrass, pigweed.

Purple Finch: *Trees and Shrubs:* White ash, sumac, juniper, elm balls, winterberry
Weeds: Ragweed.

Evening Grosbeak: *Trees and Shrubs:* Apple, mountain ash, birch, box elder, ash, sumac, conifer seeds, choke cherry
Weeds: Sunflower.

Cardinal: *Trees:* Red cedar.

Cedar Waxwing: *Trees and Shrubs:* Red cedar, apple, winterberry, mountain ash.

Pine Siskin: *Trees:* Gray birch, alder, hemlock, white pine
Weeds: Ragweed.

Tufted Titmouse: *Trees and Shrubs:* Gray birch, oak, sumac, poison ivy, bayberry.

Winter Birds of Northeast and North Central United States and Southern Canada

Swans, Geese, and Ducks
Mallard
Black Duck
Wood Duck
Common Goldeneye

Hawks, Falcons, Eagles
Cooper's Hawk
Red-tailed Hawk
Rough-legged Hawk
Sharp-shinned Hawk
American Kestrel Falcon
Gyrfalcon
Bald-headed Eagle (winter in few places where open water provides abundant fish for food)
Wild turkey
Ruffed Grouse
Ring-necked Pheasant

Gulls
Greater Black-backed Gull
Herring Gull

Pigeons, Doves
Rock Dove
Mourning Dove

Owls
Screech
Great Horned
Snowy
Barred
Saw-whet
Long-eared
Short-eared
Great Gray

Woodpeckers
Hairy
Downy
Pileated
Arctic Three-toed

Larks
Horned Lark

Jays, Crows, Ravens
Canada Jay
Blue Jay
Common Raven
Common Crow

Chickadees, Titmice
Black-capped Chickadee
Boreal Chickadee
Tufted Titmouse

Nuthatches
White-breasted Nuthatch
Red-breasted Nuthatch

Robins
Golden-crowned Kinglets
Cedar Waxwings
Northern Shrikes
House Sparrows

Blackbirds
Grackle
Brown-headed Cowbird
Starling

Buntings, Grosbeaks, Finches, Sparrows
Cardinal
Pine Grosbeak
Evening Grosbeak
Purple Finch
House Finch
Common Redpoll
Pine Siskin
Goldfinch
Red Crossbill
White-winged Crossbill
Dark-eyed Junco
Tree Sparrow
Snow Bunting
Lapland Longspur

Offshore Water Birds
Gannet
Double-crested cormorant
Greater Scaup
Oldsquaw
Common Goldeneye
Bufflehead
Red-breasted Merganser
Dovekie
Common Loon
Horned Grebe
White-winged Scoter
Surf Scoter
Common Eider
Black Guillemot

Salt Marsh Birds in Winter

Ducks
Bufflehead
Canvasback
Black Duck
Ring-necked Duck
Wood Duck
Gadwall
Barrow's Goldeneye
Common Goldeneye
Mallard
Common Merganser
Hooded Merganser
Red-breasted Merganser
Pintail

Redhead
Greater Scaup
Lesser Scaup
Shoveler
Blue-winged Teal
Green-winged Teal
American Wigeon

Hawks
Marsh
Rough-legged

Owls
Short-eared

Geese
Brant
Canada Goose
Snow Goose

Swans
Mute
Whistling

Blackbirds
Meadowlark

Crows
Common

Gulls
Great Black-backed
Herring
Laughing
Ring-billed

Sandpipers
Willet

Sparrows
Song

Visitors to Winter Bird Feeders

Blackbirds
Brown-headed Cowbird

Chickadees and Titmice
Black-capped Chickadee
Tufted Titmouse
Boreal Chickadee

Doves
Mourning

Grosbeaks, Finches, Sparrows, and Buntings
Cardinal
Purple Finch
House Finch
Goldfinch
Red Crossbill
Chipping Sparrow
Evening Grosbeak

Dark-eyed Junco
Common Redpoll
Pine Siskin
Song Sparrow
Tree Sparrow
White-throated Sparrow

Jays
Blue Jays

Mockingbirds
Mockingbird

Thrushes
Robin

Warblers
Yellow-rumped

Nuthatches
White-breasted
Red-breasted

Starlings
Starling

Weaver Finches
House Sparrow

Woodpeckers
Hairy
Downy
Pileated

Creepers
Brown Creeper

Trees of Northeast and North Central United States and Southern Canada

Conifers — Softwoods

Needles in Clusters
- White Pine
- Scotch Pine
- Red Pine
- Jack Pine
- Pitch Pine
- American Larch (Tamarack)

Flat Needles
- Balsam Fir
- Eastern Hemlock

Four-Sided Needles
- Red Spruce
- Black Spruce
- Norway
- White Spruce

Scalelike Leaves
- Northern White Cedar (Arbor Vitae)
- Atlantic White Cedar
- Red Cedar

Deciduous (Broad-Leaved) — Hardwoods

Willow Family
- Weeping Willow
- Eastern Cottonwood
- Quaking Aspen
- Bigtooth Aspen

Walnut Family
- Butternut (White Walnut)
- Black Walnut
- Pignut Hickory
- Shagbark Hickory
- Mockernut Hickory
- Bitternut Hickory

Birch Family
- Paper Birch (White Birch)
- Gray Birch
- Yellow Birch
- River Birch (Red Birch)
- Sweet Birch (Black Birch)
- Speckled Alder
- Hop Hornbeam (Ironwood)
- American Hornbeam (Blue Beech)

Beech Family
- American Beech
- American Chestnut
- White Oak
- Swamp White Oak
- Chestnut Oak
- Bur Oak
- Scrub Oak
- Black Oak
- Scarlet Oak
- Northern Red Oak

Rose Family
- Black Cherry
- Choke Cherry

- Pin Cherry (Fire Cherry)
- Wild Apple
- Mountain Ash
- Thornapple
- Shadbush

Pea Family
- Honey Locust
- Black Locust

Cashew or Sumac Family
- Staghorn Sumac
- Poison Sumac

Elm Family
- American Elm
- Slippery Elm (Red Elm)
- Cork Elm

Maple Family
- Box Elder (Ashleaf Maple)
- Sugar Maple
- Black Maple
- Silver Maple
- Red Maple
- Striped Maple (Moosewood)
- Mountain Maple

Basswood Family
- Basswood

Dogwood Family
- Alternate-leaf Dogwood
- Flowering Dogwood

Olive Family
- Red Ash
- White Ash
- Black Ash

Witch-hazel Family
- Witch-hazel

Plane-tree Family
- Sycamore (Plane-tree)

Key to Identifying Winter Water Insects

Read each pair of choices, starting with A and B. Select the best description for the insect you find. Go to the number at the end of the best description and again select the best choice before proceeding.

Adult Insects I

Those with fully developed wings (some adult water striders and marsh treaders are wingless). The wingless adult water strider usually has an abdomen as long as the thorax while the abdomen of the young is much shorter. The wingless adult marsh treader has a rigid body and a three-jointed bottom portion of the leg, while the young has a soft body and a one-jointed lower portion of the leg.

Immature Insects II

Without Fully Developed Wings (Larvae and Nymphs)

I Adult Insects

A Insects living on the surface of the water (most likely absent in winter) — 1

B Insects living under the surface of the water; free swimming — 3

1 Insects with narrow dark bodies and long legs — 2

1 Insects with oval black bodies; second and third pairs of legs very short; the first pair much longer; movements often rapid and confused: *Whirligig Beetles*

2 Second and third pairs of legs longer than the body; head much shorter than the thorax; movements quick and jerky: *Water Striders*

2 All the legs shorter than the body; head as long as the thorax; movements slow and never jerky: *Marsh Treaders*

3 Forelegs held forward in a grasping position — 4

3 Forelegs not held forward in a grasping position — 6

4 Body broad and flat — 5

4 Body long and narrow; a long, slender breathing tube on the end of the abdomen: *Waterscorpions*

5 About 2¾ inches long and 1¼ inches broad: *Larger Giant Water Bugs*

5 A little less than one inch long: *Smaller Giant Water Bugs*

6 Front wings soft and membranous — 7

6 Front wings thick and horny — 8

7 The back is shaped like the bottom of a boat and the insect swims upside down: *Backswimmers*

7 The back is flat and the insect swims right side up: *Water Boatmen*

8 Fringe on the hind legs only; color black with the sides bordered with yellow: *Diving Beetles*

8 Fringe on the second and third pairs of legs; color black, no yellow margins: *Water Scavenger Beetles*

Immature Insects

A Insects usually with wings showing as little pads on the thorax, Nymphs — 1

B Insects with no wing pads on the thorax, Larvae — 4

1 With long bristles on the end of the body — 2

1 No bristles on the end of the body — 3

2 Two bristles on the end of the body; tufts or thread-like gills at the bases of the legs: *Stonefly Nymphs*

2 Two or three bristles on the end of the body; flat leaf-like gills on the sides of the abdomen: *Mayfly Nymphs*

3 Three broad leaflike plates on the end of the body: *Damselfly Nymphs*

3 No leaflike plates on the end of the body: *Dragonfly Nymphs*

4 Without true jointed legs — 5

4 With true jointed legs — 9

5 Attached to rocks, twigs, leaves or grass in rapidly running water: *Black Fly Larvae*

5 Not attached — 6

6 Thorax larger than the remainder of the body — 7

6 Thorax not different from the remainder of the body — 8

7 End of the body forked; head smaller than the thorax: *Mosquito Larvae*

7 Two flaps on the end of the body; thorax and head very large: *Mosquito Pupae*

8 Color red; ½ to ⅔ of an inch long: *Blood Worm* (Chironomous Larvae)

8 Color dirty white or brown; 1 to 2 inches long: *Crane Fly Larvae*

9 Living in a case covered with little stones, small twigs or various kinds of debris: *Caddisfly Larvae*

9 Not living in a case — 10

10 With tapering projections on the abdomen — 11

10 No projections on the abdomen — 12

11 2 to 2½ inches long: *Dobsonfly Larvae*

11 Less than 1 inch long: *Whirligig Beetle Larvae*

12 Abdomen slender; no teeth on the strong jaws: *Water Tigers* (Diving Beetle Larvae)

12 Abdomen rather plump; teeth on the jaws: *Water Scavenger Beetle Larvae*

Suggested Further Reading

General

Buck, Margaret Waring. *In Woods and Field.* Nashville: Abingdon-Cokesbury Press, 1950.

Cosgrove, Margaret. *Wintertime for Animals.* New York: Dodd, Mead, 1975.

McClung, Robert M. "Woodlands in Winter." *Curious Naturalist.* Vol. VI, No. 6, February 1967.

Roth, Charles E. "The Field in Winter." *Curious Naturalist.* Vol. VI, No. 5, January 1967.

Stokes, Donald. *A Guide to Nature in Winter.* Boston: Little, Brown, 1977.

Chapter 1

Bentley, W. A., and W. J. Humphreys. *Snow Crystals.* New York: Dover Publications, 1931.

Frolich, R. J. "The Warmth of Snow." *Curious Naturalist.* Vol. VI, No. 5, January 1967.

Miner, Bradford, and David Miner. "How to Catch Snow Crystals." *Curious Naturalist.* Vol. II, No. 5, January 1963.

Susson, Robert F. "Snowflakes to Keep." *National Geographic.* January 1970.

CHAPTER 2

Blough, Glenn O. *Soon After September — The Story of Living Things in Winter.* New York: McGraw-Hill, 1959.

Brady, Irene. *Beaver Year.* Boston: Houghton Mifflin, 1976.

Burt, William H., and Richard P. Grossenheider. *A Field Guide to Mammals.* Boston: Houghton Mifflin Company, 1976.

George, Jean. *Snow Tracks.* New York: E. P. Dutton, 1958.

May, Charles Paul. *When Animals Change Clothes.* New York: Holiday House, 1965.

Morgan, Ann Haven. *Animals in Winter.* New York, G. P. Putnam's Sons, 1939.

Murie, Olaus J. *A Field Guide to Animal Tracks.* Boston: Houghton Mifflin, 1975.

Webster, David. *Track Watching.* New York: Franklin Watts, 1972.

CHAPTER 3

Cameron, Angus. *Nightwatchers.* New York: Four Winds Press, 1971.

Peterson, Roger Tory. *A Field Guide to the Birds.* Boston: Houghton Mifflin, 1980.

Robbins, Chandler S., Bertel Bruun, Herbert S. Zim. *Birds of North America: A Guide to Field Identification.* New York: Golden Press, 1968.

Chapter 4

Brown, Lauren. *Weeds in Winter.* New York: W. W. Norton & Co., 1976.

Metcalf, Rosamond S. *The Sugar Maple.* Canaan, N. H.: Phoenix Publishing Co., 1982.

Chapter 5

Borror, Donald, and Richard E. White. *A Field Guide to Insects.* Boston: Houghton Mifflin, 1970.

Hutchins, Ross E. *Galls and Gall Makers.* New York: Dodd, Mead, 1968.

Chapter 6

Buck, Margaret W. *Where They Go in Winter.* Nashville: Abingdon Press, 1968.

Cohen, Robert E. *Streams, Lakes, Ponds.* New York: Harper Torchbooks, 1968.

Kane, Henry. "Winter Marsh." *Curious Naturalist.* Vol. VI, No. 4, December 1966.

Massachusetts Audubon Staff. "Water." *Curious Naturalist.* Vol. VI, No. 4, December 1966.

Miner, David. "A Muskrat in a Winter Marsh." *Curious Naturalist.* Vol. VI, No. 4, December 1966.

Morgan, Ann H. *Fieldbook of Ponds and Streams.* New York: G. P. Putnam's Sons, 1930.

Russell, Helen Ross. *Winter Search Party.* New York: Thomas Nelson, 1971.

Schlegel, Mathilde. "Fishing in Winter." *Nature Study Review.* March 1918.

Chapter 7

Allison, Linda. *The Reasons for Seasons: The Great Cosmic Megagalactic Trip Without Moving from Your Chair*. Boston: Little, Brown, 1975.

Busch, Phyllis S. *A Walk in the Snow*. Philadephia: J. B. Lippincott, 1971.

Olcott, William, and R. Newton Mayall. *Field Book of the Skies*. New York: G. P. Putnam's Sons, 1954.

Osgood, William, and Leslie Hurley. *The Snowshoe Book*. Brattleboro, Vermont: Stephen Greene Press, 1971.

A Professional Resource Bibliography

Listed for many topics are several sources suggesting additional information. Each resource listed includes information to give you some idea about the content and level of understanding.

About the Source

OP — Out of print

R — Rare — May be difficult to locate

EFC — Especially for children

EFT — Especially for teachers

I — Introductory information

* — Particularly good

Ad — Advanced, in depth

AB — Activity Book

Chapter 1

Books

Abruscato, Joe, and Jack Hassard. *The Whole Cosmos.* Santa Monica: Goodyear Publishing, 1977. (EFT)

LaChapelle, Edward R. *Field Guide to Snow Crystals.* Seattle: University of Washington Press, 1969. (I/Ad)

Stecher, A., D. F. Wentworth, J. K. Couchman, and J. C. MacBean. *Snow and Ice — Examining Your Environment.* New York: Holt, 1973. (AB/EFT)

Periodicals

Blake, Charles H. "Snow Flakes and Their Patterns." *The New England Naturalist.* 1941. (R)

Palmer, E. Laurence. "The Snow Blanket." *Natural History Magazine.* January 1961. (I/Ad)

Rockcastle, Verne N. "Snow and Ice." Cornell Science Leaflet, Vol. 16, No. 2. 1968. (I/Ad)

Roth, Charles. "Snow Geology." *Curious Naturalist.* Vol. 2, No. 5, January 1963. (I)

Stong, C. L. "The Amateur Scientist." *Scientific American.* March 1966. (Ad)

Activity Folio

OBIS: Outdoor Biology Instructional Strategies. Lawrence Hall of Science, University of California, Berkeley, California 94720. (EFT)

Unit

Snow & Ice: Water & Temperature Environmental Discovery Unit. National Wildlife Federation.

Chapter 2

Books

Barker, Will. *Winter-Sleeping Wildlife.* New York: Harper & Row, 1958. (I)

Carrington, Richard. *The Mammals.* New York: Time-Life Books, 1963. (I)

Fox, Charles. *When Winter Comes.* Chicago: Reilly & Lee, 1962. (EFC)

Godin, Alfred. *Wild Mammals of New England.* Baltimore: Johns Hopkins University Press, 1977. (Ad)

Johnson, Fred. *The Foxes.* Washington, D.C.: National Wildlife Federation, 1973. (*)

Martin, Alexander, Herbert Zim, and Arnold L. Nelson. *American Wildlife and Plants — A Guide to Wildlife Food Habits.* New York: Dover Publications, 1951. (*)

Mason, George. *Animal Tracks.* New York: William Morrow, 1943. (*/R)

Pettit, Ted. *Animal Signs and Signals.* Garden City, New York: Doubleday, 1961. (I)

Roth, Charles. *An Introduction to Massachusetts Mammals.* Massachusetts Audubon Society, 1978. (I)

Periodicals

Anderson, Liz. "Jersey's Winter Mammals." *NJEA Review.* December 1972. (I)

Brownwell, L. W. "Animal Trails & Trailing." *Nature Magazine,* January 1924. (R)

Campbell, Edith. "Winter Sleepers." *Nature Study Review,* January 1918. (R)

Dawkins, M. J. R., and David Hull. "The Production of Heat by Fat." *Scientific American.* August 1967. (Ad)

Dunne, Robert. "Foxy Fox Home." *Ranger Rick.* December 1978. (EFC)

Engalls, Harry. "Wildlife Camouflage." *Highlights for Children.* April 1977. (EFC)

Goode, Emily. "Hibernation." *Curious Naturalist,* Vol. II, No. 3, November 1962. (I)

Gray, Bob. "When Winter Comes." *Ranger Rick.* December 1975. (EFC)

Hamilton, W. J. "Winter Sleep." *Audubon Nature Bulletin* and *New England Naturalist.* 1945. (R)

Irving, Laurence. "Adaptations to Cold." *Scientific American.* January 1966. (Ad)

Kelsey, Paul. "Hibernation and Winter Withdrawal." *The Conservationist.* October–November 1968. (*)

La Bastille, Anne. "How Do They Make It Through the Winter?" *National Wildlife.* December–January 1979. (I)

Letchworth, Beverly. "Where Do They Go in Winter?" *Ranger Rick.* January 1979. (EFC)

Mardsen, Catharine. "The Mystery of Hibernation." *American Red Cross Youth News.* December 1971. (EFC)

Maslowski, Karl. "The Least Weasel." *Ranger Rick.* December 1970. (EFC)

Meir, Bobby, and Joey Meir. "It's Snowshoe Time." *Ranger Rick.* February 1975. (EFC)

Mohr, Charles. "The Ways of Wildlife in Winter." *Audubon Nature Bulletin,* 1971. (I)

Palmer, E. Laurence. "He Who Runs May Be Read." *Nature Magazine,* Vol. 38, No. 10, December 1945. (*/R)

Pruitt, William O., Jr. "Animals in Snow." *Scientific American.* January 1960. (Ad)

Rockcastle, Verne N. "Animal Traces." Cornell Science Leaflet. Vol. 59, No. 2, January 1966. (I)

Roth, B. J. "A Heavy Winter Sleep." *Curious Naturalist.* January 1967. (I)

Scholander, P. F. "The Wonderful Net." *Scientific American.* April 1957. (Ad)

"Tracking." Cornell Rural School Leaflet. January 1920. (*/R)

Sherburne, Frances. "Animals in Winter." *Curious Naturalist.* Vol. I, No. 4, December 1961. (I)

Smith, Ned. "Wildlife Sketchbook — Stories in the Snow." *National Wildlife.* February–March 1979. National Wildlife Federation, Washington, DC 20036. (I)

Treat, Dorothy. "Track Stories." Audubon Nature Bulletin, Series No. 6. Bulletin No. 4. (I)

"New England Mammals in Winter." *Curious Naturalist* Supplement 42-Massachusetts Audubon Society. (I)

"Some Information on How Animals Spend Winter." *Curious Naturalist* Supplement 10-Massachusetts Audubon Society. (I)

"Track Stories in Mud, Sand & Snow." National Audubon Society Bulletin, 1952.

Charts

Animal Tracks: Footprints & Trail Patterns of 27 Common Animals. Audubon Nature Chart (14″ × 22″). (I)

Animal Tracks. National Audubon Mini-Chart (7″ × 11″). 10¢ each. (*/I)

Curriculum Kit

Animal Camouflage. Kit Guide with Structured Lesson Plans & Materials. (I)

Chapter 3

Books

Craighead, John J., and Frank C. Craighead. *Hawks, Owls, and Wildlife.* New York: Dover Publications, 1963. (I/Ad)

Dennis, John V. *A Complete Guide to Attracting Birds.* New York: Knopf, 1975. (*/I/Ad)

Griffin, Donald R. *Bird Migration.* New York: Dover Publications, 1974.

McElroy, Thomas P. *The New Handbook of Attracting Birds.* New York: Knopf, 1968. (I/Ad)

Pasquier, Roger. *Watching Birds, an Introduction to Ornithology.* Boston: Houghton Mifflin, 1977. (*/I/Ad)

Shultz, Walter. *How to Attract, House, and Feed Birds.* New York: Collier Books, 1974. (I/Ad)

Periodicals

Baynes, Ernest Harold. "Open House for Winter Birds." *Nature Magazine.* January 1923. (R)

Keil, Ernst. "Bird Guests In the Winter." *Nature Magazine.* February 1925. (R)

Morgen, Molly. "Some Cold Weather Birds of the Field." *Curious Naturalist.* February 1965. (I)

Palmer, E. Laurence. "Some Eastern Birds in Winter." *Nature Magazine,* Vol. 37, No. 16, December 1944. (**/R)

Activity Folio

Bird Feeder. Outdoor Biology Instructional Series, June 1975. University of California, Berkeley, California 94270. (EFT/I/Ad)

Unit

Audubon Flash Cards. Package of *Winter Birds* (50). (I)

Feathered Friends; Knock the Four Walls Down. P.A. Schiller, P.O. Box 307, Chicago, Illinois 60670. (EFT)

Chart

Bird Study, Bird Migration & Their Adaptations. Audubon Nature Chart (14″ × 22″). (I)

Slides

Birds. 26 Frames of Common Birds. Outdoor Pictures, Anacontes, Washington 98221.

Chapter 4

Books

Blakeslee, Albert. *Northeastern Trees in Winter.* New York: Dover Publications, 1972. (*/Ad/OP)

Campbell, Christopher, and Fay Ayland. *Winter Keys to Woody Plants of Maine.* Orono: University of Maine Press, 1975. (EFT)

Cobb, Boughton. *Field Guide to the Ferns.* Boston: Houghton Mifflin, 1963. (*)

Harlow, William. *Fruit & Twig Key to Trees & Shrubs.* New York: Dover Publications, 1972. (EFT)

Smith, Alice Upham. *Trees in a Winter Landscape.* New York: Holt, Rinehart & Winston, 1969. (*/OP)

Steele, Frederic L. *Trees and Shrubs of Northern New England.* 1971. Society for the Protection of New Hampshire Forests, 5 State Street, Concord, New Hampshire. (*/I)

Symonds, George W. D. *The Tree Identification Book. The Shrub Identification Book.* New York: William Morrow & Co., 1958, 1963. (*/I)

Trelease, William. *Winter Botany.* New York: Dover Publications, 1931. (*/OP)

Periodicals

"Common Trees & Their Twigs." National Audubon Society, December 1962. (I)

"Clues for Twig Detectives." *Curious Naturalist* Suppl. 6 — Mass. Audubon Society, December 1962. (I)

Parker, Johnson. "Cold Resistance in Woody Plants." *The Botanical Review,* Vol. 29, No. 2, April–June 1963. (Ad)

Rockcastle, Verne N. "Winter Things." Cornell Science Leaflet, Vol. 58, No. 2, January 1965. (*)

Sakai, A., and C. J. Weiser. "Freezing Resistance of Trees in North America with Reference to Tree Regions." *Ecology*, Vol. 54, 1973. (Ad)

Vasilyev, I. M. "Winter of Plants." American Institute of Biological Science, 1961. J. Levitt, ed. (Ad)

Weiser, C. J. "Cold Resistance and Injury in Woody Plants." *Science*. September 1970. (Ad)

Chart

Evergreens and Twigs of Common Trees. National Audubon Miniature Chart (7" × 11") 10¢ each. (I)

Identified Common North American Evergreens. Audubon Nature Charts. (I)

Twigs of Common Trees. Audubon Nature Charts (14" × 22"). (I)

Activity Investigation

Movekit — Winter Trees & Twigs. Regional Center for Education Training, Montshine Museum, Hanover, New Hampshire. (*)

Tree Silhouettes; Buds & Twigs; How to be a Twig Detective; Knock the Four Walls Down. P.A. Schiller and Associates, P.O. Box 307, Chicago, Ill. 60670. (EFT)

Chapter 5

Books

Couchman, J. S. *Small Creatures.* Minneapolis: Mine Publishing, Inc., 1971. (*/AB)

Felt, Ephraim. *Plant Galls and Gall Makers.* New York: Hafner Press, 1965. (Ad/EFT)

Frost, S. W. *Insect Life and Insect Natural History.* New York: Dover Publications, 1942. (*)

Periodicals

Brynton, K. S. "Life in a Snowbank." *Yankee.* February 1974. (I)

Fischer, Richard B. "The Curious World of Plant Galls." *Audubon Nature Bulletin.* 1956. (*/I)

Fischer, Richard B. "Lumps, Bumps, and Clumps." *Ranger Rick.* December 1974. (EFC)

Fischer, Richard B. "Some Plant Galls of New York." *The Conservationist.* February–March 1964. (*)

MacNamara, Charles. "Insects of the Snow." *Nature Magazine.* December 1925. (*/R)

Palmer, E. Laurence. "Common Galls of Woody Plants." *Nature Magazine.* Vol. 40, No. 6, June–July 1947. (*/R)

Welch, Paul. "Aquatic Insects." *National Student Review.* April 1912. (*/R)

Wyatt, Jean. "The No Good Tree." *Ranger Rick.* August 1978. (EFC)

Chapter 6

Periodicals

Kane, Henry. "Winter Marsh." *Curious Naturalist.* Vol. VI, No. 4, December 1966. (*/I)

Massachusetts Audubon Staff. "Water." *Curious Naturalist.* Vol. VI, No. 4, December 1966. (*/I)

Miner, David. "A Muskrat in a Winter Marsh." *Curious Naturalist.* Vol. VI, No. 4, December 1966. (*/I)

Schlegel, Mathilde. "Fishing in Winter." *Nature Study Review.* March 1918. (*/R)

CHAPTER 7

Books

Mahoney, Russ. *Wintering.* Harrisburg, Pa.: Stockpole Books, 1976. (I)

Rogers, Barbara Radcliffe. *Yankee Home Crafts.* Dublin, New Hampshire: Yankee, Inc., 1979. (I)

Rulstrum, Calvin. *Paradise Below Zero.* New York: Collier Books, 1968. (EFT)

Periodical

Harris, James T. "Snow Trails." *Blair & Ketchum's Country Journal.* February 1976.

GENERAL

Sources listed here include literature, field guides, and other publications. They contain information about winter ecology that includes topics contained in more than one chapter.

Books

Beston, Henry. *Northern Farm.* New York: Ballantine Books, 1948. (*)

Buck, Margaret Waring. *In Woods and Field.* Nashville: Abingdon-Cokesbury Press, 1950. (*/EFC)

Cosgrove, Margaret. *Wintertime for Animals.* New York: Dodd, Mead, 1975. (*/EFC)

Hustre, Janet. *Nature Study for Infants.* 1969, Thomas Nelson & Sons, Coperwood and Davis Streets, Camden, NJ 08103. (EFT)

Leopold, Aldo. *A Sand County Almanac.* New York: Oxford University Press, 1949. (*)

Nickelsburg, Janet. *Nature Activities for Early Childhood.* Reading, Massachusetts: Addison-Wesley, 1976. (EFT)

Quinn, John R. *The Winter Woods.* Greenwich, Connecticut: The Chatham Press, 1976. (*)

Russell, Helen Ross. *Winter — A Field Trip Guide.* Boston: Little, Brown, 1972. (I)

Stecher, A., D. F. Wentworth, J. K. Couchman, and J. C. MacBean. *Your Senses — Examining Your Environment.* New York: Holt, 1973. (EFT/AB)

Stokes, Donald. *A Guide to Nature in Winter.* Boston: Little, Brown, 1977. (**/I)

Teale, Edwin Way. *Wandering Through Winter.* New York: Dodd, Mead, 1957. (*)

Periodicals

McClung, Robert M. "Woodlands in Winter." *Curious Naturalist.* Vol. VI, No. 6, February 1967. (I)

Phares, Ross. "When the Food Runs Out." *Ranger Rick.* October 1970. (EFC)

Roth, Charles E. "The Field in Winter." *Curious Naturalist.* Vol. VI, No. 5, January 1967. (I)

Roth, Charles E. "Shivering Tale." *Curious Naturalist.* Vol. IX, No. 5, January 1970. (I)

"Winter," *Curious Naturalist* Quarterly Magazine. 1976, 1977, 1978, 1979/80. (*)

Pamphlet

"Resources for Teachers." Sierra Club, 530 Bush Street, San Francisco, California. (EFT)

Unit

"Knock the Four Walls Down: A Guide to Winter Ecological Study." Nick Rodes and P. J. Anundson, P.A. Schiller and Associates, P.O. Box 307, Chicago, Ill. (EFT)

Charts

Forest Food Chains. Audubon Nature Charts (14″ × 22″).

Forest Food Chains. Miniature Charts (7″ × 11″) 10¢ each.

Slides

"Lure of Winter" Plants and Animals in Winter. Outdoor Pictures, Anacontes, Washington 98221.

Activity Folio

Gaming in the Outdoors. Sensory Hi-Lo Hunt. Outdoor Biology Instructional Series. (I)

Index